The Chronicles of the Sacred Rulix Crystal

Book One

The Spiral Society

Uzoma Peter Lane

1

A publication of The Pocket Revolution-First Edition

ISBN: 978-0-6151-9776-0

Printed in the United States of America.

Table of Contents

Extra Chronicles

About the Author

Uzoma Peter Lane was born in 1983 and immediately developed a passion for writing. At three years of age he had mastered reading, and three years later, began work on his first story, called The Chronicles of Silver, as an outlet for the problems at school. Over the years he has written over three hundred poems, several short stories, and articles for local newspapers throughout the DC Metro area. His poetry is featured in several anthologies including Poetry by Moonlight.

He currently resides in the District's fourth ward where he is earning a degree in history Howard University. Uzoma aspires to become a professor, and weave his stories into one epic series.

Dedicated to Isadore and Ihuaku Lane, whose tireless efforts have paid for the talent here displayed.

This book would be impossible without twenty-four years of encouragement, support and tuition payments.

Thank you kindly, and live well always and forever.

The Rulix Crystal...

A king did lead the Five of Right,
into the wood by pale moonlight.
To sift Melinda's will and bone,
who once did kneel nigh King Ihon.

The scattered rose that forged his power,
increased her fortunes every hour.
When once the servant comes to rule,
the stars must shine upon a duel.

In Voligdoes she placed her hope,
as Ihon wound the hangman's rope.
Know ye the light within the Cryst,
reduced six realms to ash and mist

----MERI Record AL47 "Silver Lore"
Compiled by: Dr. X. A. Talbot

Prologue: The Wicked Oppressing

Warm, crimson light cut across the room, veiled in the mysterious notes of a very old carol. Drawn by the melody, a peach skinned toddler tore across the carpets at top speed, his golden hair glinting in the fanciful sunlight. He knew nothing of the ravenous frost that tore at innocent flesh just beyond his festively decorated windows, for all that concerned him was the impossibly beautiful tower of light before him. It was a pure wonder, like something that belonged in a fairy tale. Spangled with multicolored lights that resembled tiny fireflies in the darkness, it called to the young boy's heart, positively pleading to be touched. Obediently, he stretched out one chubby little hand and prepared to clasp the wondrous light when, all at once, he began to rise away from the treasure he sought.

"You mustn't break that" rang a high, melodic voice, "not yet anyway." Caramel colored hands turned the small child so that he beheld his mother's oval face. Annoyed at being robbed of a glorious experience, he frowned, sticking out his bottom lip.

"Well I'm sorry Alexander!" she replied, laughing harder, "but Christmas trees are very fragile. How about that instead?" she asked pointing with a flourish to something on the beige sofa to their right.

When Alexander saw it, his eyes grew wide with longing and his heart leapt as he shouted "Teddy!" for all to hear. "You're welcome" she said smiling, and placed him on the ground. Moments later, Alexander had a white, cotton soft, teddy with a satin-like ribbon in a bear hug.

With a light heart, Alexander's mother turned toward the kitchen but she'd only gone three steps before Alexander caught her leg in a grateful one-armed hug.

"I love you too, Alexander" she responded, kneeling to hug him properly, "and Merry Christmas!" she cried, ruffling his hair.

This had been Alma Lightarrow's third happy holiday and she was beginning to get used to it. She thought less and less of the horrors she had once endured and was finally beginning to feel secure. As she watched her son struggle to name his new friend, she reflected that her pursuers had apparently lost her trail.

"Thank God" she whispered meaningfully, smiling brightly as a pair of keys chimed from the other side of their apartment door. At once, Alexander tucked his teddy bear under his arm like a football and dashed for the door in time to collide with his square jawed, snow covered father.

"Guess who's back?" he cried, shaking snow from his gray trench coat.

"Daddy!" Alexander exclaimed, clutching his father's damp pant-leg tightly. Alma placed a warm kiss on one of her husband's smooth cheeks and he turned to her with a warm smile as he swept his son into his arms.

"Long day!" he laughed, kissing Alma's full lips, "Long day indeed. Worth it for you two though" he finished, placing his fedora on Alexander's head. It proved to be far too large, and covered the child's eyes quite well. At once, he let out an alarmed squeal that drew a chuckle from his father.

"He's still scared of the dark" Alma noted needlessly as she "rescued" her son.

One of a growing number of people forced to work on Christmas, Detective Peter Lightarrow and his partner Christopher Allen, had spent the day hunting down the elusive Bloodied Saints. A terrifying band of cold-blooded terrorists, the Saints seemed to have a special affinity for the city of Miriam. Only a week ago two sections of a city government building had begun smoking and burst into flames. Peter had spent many hours in the ashy ruins gathering evidence that day. To make matters worse, the Saints had their converts. It had been determined that their anti-government philosophy had influenced John Turner to kill a fellow citizen in 1961. That piece of information had made a priority out of what was originally thought to be a close-knit group of foreign anarchists.

Peter, however, was no longer concerned with any of that. His bald head and sharp features ensured that he almost always looked like the hard boiled detective he was, but once he entered his apartment the so called "Hellfighter" became a gentle giant. An hour had passed and he was now engaged in trotting around the living room on all fours, Alexander giggling happily on his back, still clutching his new teddy bear, named Melvin. This gentle nature was what had attracted Anna to him in the first place and as she saw it on display, swift currents coursed through her all over again.

She would never have believed it but her life was beginning to resemble a fairy tale.

"Perhaps" she mused to herself, "we'll finally live happily ever after."

After several more games of "Cowboy", Peter carried his son to bed where the usual bribe of milk and cookies waited on a nightstand, praying that the little one was tuckered out. He left a butterfly-shaped night light to guard against the darkness, and finally prepared to relax and enjoy his Christmas.

Across from the Jennings Apartments the next morning, children dashed in and out of the arcade adjacent the Chinese carry-out, spending as much of their Christmas money saving the world as time would allow. A light wind bore still more snow to the ground in lazy spirals and, occasionally, one or two cars cruised down Weeping Willow Lane. Amid the cascading, wintry blanket, a young, blond haired woman plodded tiredly towards the city's library. She wore a holiday themed hat under the hood of her thick beige coat, which was accompanied by a tightly knotted scarf and red mittens. One of those mittens held a hand connected to a smaller child frequently referred to as Nicholas.

Not much older than eight, he seemed to be allowing himself to be dragged along. His face twisted with confusion, he asked his sister a question for the millionth time,

"Where're we going, Emilie? You said you'd tell me today so spill."

The woman shook visibly on hearing her name. Few people remembered it anymore. She had steeped her soul in darkness for so long that the trappings of her old life seemed alien to her.

"Be patient and you'll know soon" she replied kindly, but she wished she were wrong.

"Why now?" she thought miserably to herself. He had been under her care for years now, always looking just as she found him. Nicholas hadn't grown an inch taller or a day older in five years, so Emile had been certain this day would come. She had dreaded it above all else as she conducted the business she was forced to undertake, and each morning, as she glanced upon his sleeping form, she prayed her masters had not discovered what he was. But on the sixty-sixth floor of the dark tower they lived in, nothing remained hidden long.

Emilie had been in Miriam for three days working up the courage to do her job. She had spent many hours with inexplicable tears freezing upon her cheeks. Nightmares had invaded her sleep that prominently featured Nicholas laughing madly in pools of someone else's blood. She didn't want to do this to him but she was afforded very little choice.

Today her eyes were permanently crossed as she continued aimlessly down the lane, her purse crammed full of the knick-knacks she had distracted Nicholas with yesterday. They had spent the holiday in a cheap motel being comforted by overdoses of television and ice cream. The child's persistent question rang in her mind as clearly as it had in her ears.

"Why can't we go home?" it asked.

"Because we'd be killed" Emilie thought, but to Nicholas, she said nothing.

High above her, veiled in mysterious, often whimsical clouds, and thick curtains of snow, a hard faced young man sailed the skies. Neither the wind nor the bitter cold seemed to faze him in the least. He simply soared through it all standing ramrod straight, as if he were made of stone. The joyful shouts of the children below meant nothing to him. Joy was an emotion he had abandoned long ago.

His eyes mechanically searched the landscape below, endlessly following the same target. He had grown up here once upon a time. He had read in the library to which Emilie drew ever closer, dashed down these very wintry streets, and laughed louder than any child of Odine County's more affluent families ought. Yet none of that mattered now. Despite the dazzling height he had attained, he could clearly see the troubled look on Emilie's face. He noted the tears building behind her eyelashes with a bitter frown, and glanced upon Nicholas' face looking for signs of fear. He found none.

"He hasn't been told yet" he growled to himself, "the girl's wasting valued time."

At once, he stopped moving and vanished in a pulse of white light. A split second later, Emilie yelped in shock and fear as the man appeared before her. He wore a full body suit of form fitting, metallic, white armor that seemed to be alive. It quivered every few seconds and seemed to make the surrounding snow look dingy by comparison. Long braids of jet black hair fell to his shoulders to resemble nothing more than the shadow of a lion's mane. Terrified, Nicholas caught Emilie's leg in a stranglehold causing her another shock.

"It's all right, little brother" she whispered, but she wasn't so sure.

Daniel stared coldly at the woman before him, who began to weep, as snowflakes settled on his dark skin. He looked thoroughly unimpressed with the spectacle, but his heart was in bitter pain.
"I wanted to help these people" he thought miserably, "the power to help…" his thoughts trailed away.

There was no help he could offer now, after all, barring death. Shaking his dreads free of snow, he snatched up young Nicholas who let loose an ear-piercing scream nobody heard. Like most of their kind, Nicholas had learned to fear Daniel at an early age, and for very good reason.

"At your urging" Daniel intoned darkly, "the Spiral Society has babysat this Element for ten years. In that time, he has been the only resident of Inverness not called upon to perform the task for which we are assembled. Our Director can tolerate this arrangement no longer. That is why you are here. Dr. Forester gave you orders to supervise this boy's first assignment. However, you seem reluctant to comply."

With cruel skill, he twisted the boy's arms painfully behind his back. He locked an armored hand around one of Nicholas' wrists and began squeezing forcefully, eliciting fresh screams of pain.

"No!" Emilie screamed bitterly, "Leave him alone!" The snow-capped street beneath Daniel began to glow dangerously. But the young man reacted instantly, crossing two fingers and moving them in a downward slash. At once, soundlessly, a coal black chunk of flaming hail slammed into Emilie's stomach, igniting her coat and knocking her to the ground.

Shrieking soundlessly, she rolled about in the snow, desperately trying to extinguish herself. The ground beneath Daniel returned to normal without incident and he hurled young Nicholas on top of his sister.

"Be thankful that he's more useful to Forester alive." Daniel growled menacingly. "Still, he will be utterly useless if his assignment isn't complete in 18 hours." With that, he vanished once more, leaving the siblings to cry for different reasons. As soon as the fire died, Nicholas fearfully asked,

"What am I supposed to do?"

The Bloodied Saints were continuing to occupy Peter's time so Alma only had her dear friend Hannah to take down the decorations with. The two had been friends since time immemorial, sharing the highs and lows of life, along with its bitter secrets.

In college, Hannah had dedicated her life to medicine, and she now practiced as a nurse, as far removed from her New England home as she could get. Bright eyed and cheerful, she worked quickly, stripping the tree of lights and baubles. Whenever one of her hands was free, Alexander would take it into his tiny clutches and sing "Rowan, Rowan!" at the top of his voice. Each time she would giggle; sometimes she kissed his hands. Ever since she had confided her middle name, it was all he would call her.

"You sure he didn't eat too many candy canes, Alma?" she jokingly asked after the sixth such interruption.

"Yup" Alma laughed, tickling her son's chin. As he burst into gurgled laughter, Alna began singing her favorite hymn.

"The wicked oppressing" her voice rang melodically, "now cease from distressing. Sing praises to His name..."

"He forgets not his own" Hannah finished.

She hummed the song twice more, thinking of the terrible life she had escaped at the hands of a gaggle of scientists. Her mind and body had been viciously tortured, but more importantly, she had been cursed with power. Since her escape she had hidden the remarkable abilities that had secured her freedom, certain that they would betray her. Even now, happily singing beside her laughing son, she was certain she would keep the secret to her dying day. Only Hannah had been trusted with the true story of her disappearance ever so long ago, the pain, the torture, and the powers they had won her. Her husband knew nothing and she hoped he always would. As for Alexander, the only secrets she meant to share with him were scrawled in a journal she had written long ago.

Night fell and Peter returned ready and willing to leave his troubles at the door. Spying Hannah, he called out teasingly,

"Well if it ain't Nurse Bennett. What a surprise. I didn't know you all still made house calls" he laughed.

"Hello to you too" she replied, mock offense in her voice, "how goes the Elliot Ness impersonation?"

"Not so well" Peter answered, shaking with glee, "they're beginning to notice I'm black!"

Everyone laughed at that, and dinner was served. Highlights included a stellar attack on the brownie bowl by Alexander. Hannah was still cleaning fudge from his cheeks when the bell rang. For an instant, craven fear gripped Alma.

"They've found me at last!" she thought to herself, but as the ring repeated she buried the thought. "Assassins don't ring door bells" she told herself, and with a bit of effort, she answered the door.

Drenched in tears and white as a sheet, Nicholas stood before her, shaking violently.

"I'm really sorry" he gurgled, raising his right hand, and Alma realized what he meant to do too late. A golden beam of light shot through her heart and the child dashed down the hall with inhuman speed as Alma fell silently to the floor. Nicholas dived into the stairwell but that didn't spare him from the anguished wails that filled the hall as Peter rushed to the door and discovered his wife.

Emilie advanced stoically down the hall, silencing Peter with a second golden beam. She slipped passed him and quickly spotted young Alexander who had begun to cry at all the noise. Sighing deeply, she approached him.

"For what I must do, I apologize" she breathed, and bent to kidnap the child.

However, Hannah had other ideas.

"Harm him at your peril!" she screamed, leaping in Emilie's way. Hannah lunged at the invader's throat, only to be hoisted into the air by unseen forces and unceremoniously slammed into the nearest wall.

Emilie caught the struggling toddler around the middle and prepared to leave the dismal scene she had created, when Nicholas returned, fire in his tear-stained eyes.

"If you do this" he said slowly, "I'll never love you again. I..I'll hate you forever and never speak to you again. He's just a little kid" the child finished, sobbing. And, once again, he was gone.

Sighing deeply, Emilie released Alexander at once, shaken to her core. She could do without her life, but she needed her brother's love. She heard Hannah stirring as she joined Nicholas in the hall. They said nothing to each other, but simply began running, trying not to think of the fallen angel hiding in the clouds. In her heart, Emilie prayed that they might elude death as long as Alma had.

Barely conscious, Hannah lay bleeding against the wall as a panicked three year old called her name over and over again. The noise eventually sparked the curiosity of Alma's neighbor Dottie Jenkins. When she took in the scene the old woman nearly killed herself diving for the phone.

Police later concluded that the assailants had been recruits of the Bloodied Saints whose purpose had been to punish the Lightarrow family for conducting investigations against them. Further investigation was promised, but Hannah found no comfort in that. In the days that followed she nearly went insane with grief as Alexander asked for his parents without end.

Emilie and Nicholas ran for months, never staying in one place for more than an hour. So far, it seemed, they had been lucky, but neither of them wanted to rest. Hidden in the clouds above, a dark shadow noted their every move. Neither wind nor cold seemed to faze it, but that phantom knew its own pain.

Chapter One: A Hope in Sorrow

Dawn had come again to the city of Miriam, to Weeping Willow Lane, and to a shadowy bedroom. Weak, beams of sunlight played upon the sleeping face within. That face was pinched in the hollow anger of bitter dreams. The boy to whom it belonged was twisting violently between his blankets as if he were being pelted with burning coals. He was drenched in a spreading wave of sweat and the cotton pajamas he wore had become plastered against his slight frame. Swift, sure footsteps could be heard pounding ever closer as the child's fevered murmurs turned to the desperate screams children usually reserve for impossibly dire situations. His movements seemed to grow more brutal with each passing second and he began to tear at the air as his screams grew louder still. The door banged open just as the curtains came off their rod in shreds. A silhouette was immediately visible in the light that spilled from the hall. It dived for the bed, tearing away the sheets the child was tangled in. The child struggled fiercely against this apparition until his eyes shot open in blind terror to behold his guardian's face.

"These nightmares have got to stop" she cried softly, and with a great effort, she freed her charge from his blankets.

The shouting died away at once, replaced by rivulets of bitter tears. His chest heaving with emotion, he fell into his guardian's waiting arms. She rocked him gently, tears staining her hospital scrubs, and soon the crying turned to hiccups, and a single word.

"Rowan?" he sobbed with every breath, "Ro-r-rowan?" Each time it was a question, as if he doubted his guardian was real.

"It's all right" she replied, "its all right. I'm right here. It's okay." She rocked him a few minutes more and, as always, he fell silent.

"Good morning, Alexander" she sighed, and helped him into fresh clothes.

The nightmares began a year ago but each was the same as the last. A sleek and powerful jaguar with eyes like yellow moons would stalk young Alexander through stinging winds and choking fog. He would run barefoot over jagged stones, tear his clothes on hidden barbs, and scream in the purest terror as vipers struck at his heels in unending currents. Above, wine-red spirals would pierce the clouds and when Alexander strayed beneath these it felt as if thousands of needles had been driven into his soul at once.

He had learned to fear sleep above all else but it could not be avoided. The first morning had been unbearable, and in the weeks to come, the woman he called Rowan tried everything she knew. But no amount of hot chocolate or medicine seemed to work. Each morning held the same feral screams.

This morning, Alexander ate in silence. Rowan didn't even bother trying to start a conversation this time. Each day she would build up her hopes only to suffer another agonizing disappointment.

At first, she thought he was being rude and punished him accordingly, but after several days, she sought the help of her colleagues. But no one could solve the mystery of Alexander's silence so she sat before the glorified card table they used for dining, and watched as the child ate his cereal. Alexander's movements were deliberate. Almost mechanically, the spoon found his mouth each time, but he might have been eating sand for all the difference it made to him. He kept his eyes focused on the woman before him, whose proper name was Hannah Bennett. He was only eight but he knew enough to recognize anguish and frustration in his guardian's eyes.

For the first few weeks, he had tried to speak but his throat felt as if daggers tore at its lining. No sound ever came through, but his every attempt brought him hours of fierce suffering. Eventually, he had given up, and his voice could only be heard each morning crying "Rowan", the last word he had left.

Hannah leapt out of her reverie as a miniature grandfather clock struck eight.

"I'm going to be late!" she cried in a voice that was only slightly flustered, and she crossed the table to catch Alexander in a quick one-armed hug. "Don't take any shortcuts to school, be on your best behavior, and call me if you need anything" she panted. She bent to deliver a peck of a kiss to Alexander's forehead, but missed her mark and ended up with strands of pillowy, golden brown hair on her lips. As she snatched up her equipment and dashed for the door, she got a rare treat. Behind her, she heard her unfortunate young charge clearly trying to hold back laughter. It sounded no better than a faint whisper, but that didn't matter. Her heart seemed to swell, and she dropped the dark leather relic of a nurse's bag she carried and rushed to his side. Moments later she was tickling him without mercy and his expression had become a vision of rapturous joy. But soon, her eyes fell to the carrying case she had discarded and she broke into a sort of stooping run in order to swipe it up without losing time.

"Have a nice day Alexander!" she called as she tore the front door open, and in a moment, she was gone.

Joy quickly fled Alexander's face. His forced silence had made his world seem far emptier than it was. He hated to be alone with his memories of the night before, and the thought of vipers and spirals almost made him eager to get to school. Almost. Most people think of school as a place to learn and make friends. They assume it's a controlled environment where children can foster friendships and work together in peace. Alexander knew better. His school was a waking nightmare. For years, Alexander had attended Sunrise Elementary School with only one goal in mind: to someday make a friend. Instead, his days were spent dodging hordes of bullies, and something much fouler.

He rose slowly from his seat, almost collapsing one of the shaky, wooden legs. A moment later he was in the apartment's tiny kitchen staring at peeling custard-colored paint as he rinsed his cereal bowl. The floor beneath him became wet almost immediately and Alexander made a note to mention the leaky pipes that evening. Then memory hit him like a furious wind and he wiped his hands and, fishing a small notepad from his pocket, tore out a sheet and scrawled a note. He stuck it on their ancient refrigerator on his way back to the dining room and snatched up the small book bag Hannah had placed there earlier. With a heave the bag was slung across his shoulder and he stepped into the hall to begin his march toward another day of unmitigated suffering.

The hallways of the Jennings Apartment Complex were badly lit. Every so often a fluorescent light that seemed to be flickering through its last throes provided just enough of a beam to see by. Several of these beacons were missing their covers and sported stained and discolored bulbs. Halfway across this gloom, Alexander passed a woman whose skin had grayed with age. She stood before her door in a stained lace nightgown, a ratty pink housecoat, and bunny slippers with missing ears. Her hair was one ghastly shock of white, and her eyes bored into the child with bare hatred.

"S'help me I'mma git your screaming behind outta this place one day!" she called after him. "Ever' morning's the same thing. C'mere boy lemme beat all that hollerin outta ya."

She screamed hoarsely and dived after Alexander in a tipsy little shuffle but by then he had reached the stairwell. Without a word, he dived inside and both of them knew the old woman stood no chance of catching him. She continued to stand in the hall grumbling ferociously to herself.

"Old" Dottie Jenkins wasn't the only neighbor with complaints about Alexander's nightmares. Indeed, just a week ago, the landlord had arrived to threaten Hannah with eviction citing thirteen complaints of "intolerably disruptive noise". It had taken an hour of garnering sympathy for Alexander to keep from being thrown into the street. As he marched down the Spartan staircase, his miserable sentiments were joined by guilt. Someday the two of them would end up sleeping in Arcadia

Park, across from the school, and it would be entirely his fault. With a deep sigh he shoved the heavy door before him and emerged in a deceptively elegant lobby.

The road to Sunrise was easy and painless for most. As one came out of the apartment, he would turn right and walk straight for about four blocks. He'd pass another three-story apartment complex, the middle school, and the police station on his right, and the dry cleaners, a Chinese carryout and a mini-mart on his left. At the police station, he'd simply cross the street to the library and turn right to arrive at the entrance to the school's playground. But, for Alexander, things were never simple. His route would begin at the edge of the wood that bordered the parking lot behind the apartments. Here he parted waves of overhanging branches whose leaves shielded the entrance like a curtain.

The path beyond was shaded by a canopy of impressive oak trees and Alexander entered the cool darkness with a sense of relief. With the grace of an expert, he stepped past barely visible barbs and brambles, glancing to his right every few moments to make sure he wasn't lost. A cacophony of insects chirped out of sight just as Alexander spotted a small stream to his right. At once, he became fiercely alert. Now came the most difficult part of his chosen route. The trees became denser and the path narrower. Soon the wood had become a solid wall on Alexander's left. The child shook badly as the road began to rise sharply but he managed to reign in his growing panic. When Alexander finally stood eight feet above the rocky stream with nothing to hold on to, he began crying silently, filled with a heavy anger. At any moment, he could slip from this narrow perch and shatter the bones in his body, or drown beneath the muddy water. Children throughout the Jennings Apartments had been warned against it time and again, with horrid stories of unwary children's disappearances and much harsher disciplines, but Alexander had no choice. For him, the easy way was barred.

Fear is not always an easy lesson to learn. Quite often, pride and ego interfere with what should be an incredibly simple judgment. Thus, Alexander had borne the perils of the normal route for a year before it finally sank in. Each morning, he had dashed across the sidewalks, dodging a clandestine hail of sharp rocks hurled with a sniper's accuracy. More than once, they had scarred his arms and lodged in his head, leaving bloody craters. Hannah, the local police, and Amanda Phillips, Sunrise's principal, had tried to discover the culprits but their efforts proved to be in vain and were rendered unnecessary when Alexander discovered his perilous new route. The rocks were followed by merciless taunting and spiteful attacks, but Alexander showed up every morning just the same. He believed it his right to be able to choose a route to school and he did not intend to let himself be deterred by bullies. Then, one cold December morning, Alexander learned his lesson.

That morning, like many before it, Hannah had left for work in a fit of hysterical tears. Between her immense workload, the nightmares, and his endless silence, she was slowly losing control of her emotions. Seeing his only guardian in such a state had branded Alexander with guilt, and on the walk to Sunrise, his heart seemed to slip toward his shoes. The wind was a menace and slashed Alexander's peach-like skin until his eyes watered with pain. And it was in the teary blur and stinging wind that he saw it. At once his heart tried to rip a hole in his chest. His entire body quaked savagely and feral instincts screamed within his mind. Acid seemed to swell like a geyser in his chest, and he vomited loudly as his legs gave up the ghost. He tried to call out for help and was rewarded with such miserable pain that his face twisted in anguish and he slammed his fist into the ground. Before him lay a pretty girl his own age sporting crisp blue eyes and auburn hair. She wore a navy-blue and white dress woven with lace and covered in elegant images of hummingbirds. She lay in the cold unmoving, and covered in wide gashes and a sickly gray-red blood. Alexander had begun to back away in craven fear when he passed out from sheer terror, and ever since, he'd been balancing between a wall of trees and a steep fall.

Just as the path became so narrow that Alexander had to shuffle his feet to keep from falling, it swept to the left through a gap in the trees.

"Finally!" Alexander thought, and carefully followed the road uphill to its destination: Arcadia Park.

Verdant fields and crisp blue skies greeted anyone lucky enough to visit the aptly named playground. It contained an exercise center, a baseball diamond, a basketball court, picnic areas, and all the standard playground equipment a kid could ask for. Even the terrifying memory of a nameless little girl could not dampen the sheer joy the park inspired in children everywhere. Alexander's guilt and terror vanished without a trace and the only weight he was carrying now lay in his book bag.

He was tempted to stay here all day. After all, he would be home long before Hannah was and she'd never know a thing. It was also quite certain that the happiness he felt would evaporate the moment he set foot in Sunrise. A day in the park would have been a dream come true but Alexander marched resolutely toward the park's proper entrance. For all its woes, he knew Sunrise held something so wonderful it put even Arcadia's wonders to shame.

Sunrise and Arcadia Park were bisected by a dead end street placed there primarily to funnel traffic into the Miriam City Library parking lot beside the school. Alexander crossed at a solemn pace that might have been dangerous if more people read on Monday mornings. On the other side a wild collection of trees bordered a walkway comprised of wide, wooden steps. Alexander took these to the fence that marked the end of Sunrise's play area, and with a sigh, he marched across the low cut grass toward the four-story nightmare ahead.

Inside Alexander marched past the morning and afternoon kindergarten classes, which were plastered with wild sketches and macaroni art. The pictures conjured unpleasant memories of solitude and loneliness. Ignoring a returning feeling of hopeless sorrow, he started up the green, carpeted ramps that led to each bank of classrooms. At Sunrise, each grade had four classrooms. Each room was designed to hold twenty-eight children, but sometimes, thirty or more were accepted. Alexander crossed the ramp that led to the school's third grade bank and entered the second classroom on the left.

The second the door shut behind him, Alexander dived for his cubby and deposited his heavy book bag. From the top shelf, he procured a thick but functional pair of glasses and lovingly put them on. Since the rock attacks had begun, Alexander made a habit of leaving his glasses in his cubby where they were safe from damage. He meant to find a seat in front of the classroom's three octagonal tables, but as he turned, a fist caught him in the stomach.

"Hello, Mouse" said his attacker, in a crisp English accent. Alexander folded over in pain, eyes watering behind his glasses. He recognized the faded blue jeans of April Rainer, a vicious brat who had bullied Alexander since the first grade.

"I should have stayed at the park" he thought bitterly. But it was too late for regrets so Alexander tried to stand and face his foe.

"Oh no you don't" April cried, and with a swift motion, she caught his woolly hair in her hands. April yanked with all her might, her brow furrowing with the effort. At once, Alexander was rocked by mindless pain.

Surprisingly, April's grip was like a vise, and Alexander was sure he'd be bald if he didn't react soon. His face grew red as he struggled against what felt like walls of scalding air. He commanded his arms to move and they did so very gradually, as if they were suddenly weighted with lead. After what seemed like eternities, his hands were finally in position and he caught April's wrist with all the force he could muster. A tug of war commenced with Alexander pulling toward himself and trying to free his hair, and April unrelentingly resisting.

The pain in Alexander's head had now past unbearable and he began to kick and squirm violently, as if he were being electrocuted. April smiled down at him pitilessly.

"Gonna squeak, Mouse?" she teased. In response, Alexander forced all of his will into a punch and caught April in her jaw. April flew back in disbelief, releasing her captive more from shock than anything else. One of the reasons April loved to tease Alexander was that he could be counted on never to fight back. Alexander did not observe the outrage on her face as he fell to the floor in a heap. The migraine marching across his mind like a conquering army was far too great. April, however, recovered in a flash, ready to take revenge for her aching jaw.

Without a second thought, she landed a stellar kick in Alexander's stomach. Fire swelled hatefully in his chest as every ounce of air spewed out of his body.

"That's what you get for punching me!" she cried victoriously. And with a venomous glare, she turned to leave.

By this time, Alexander's classmates began to flock to the source of the commotion. This was unfortunate for April because as she took her first step, Alexander pulled her ankle with enough force to cause her to trip. April yelped in surprise and was soon surrounded by her mirthful peers. At the head of the pack was the rust haired "Wild" Bill Wildre. Bill was a legend at Sunrise. His aptitude for troublemaking had won him many allies and followers. Rumor had it that during his first weeks in kindergarten, he was suspended twice for attempting to make fireballs with paper and matches. As time passed, his antics grew in scale and creativity so that one occasion the school had to be evacuated. Bill stared at Alexander with a mischievous grin etched upon his face. As their eyes met, Alexander tensed visibly and struggled to gain his feet.

But Bill leaned in with the blinding speed of a hawk and snatched Alexander's glasses from his face in one smooth motion.

"You wont be needing these" Bill laughed, waving the thick, metal frames in the air, "so I'll just get rid of them for you".

The class broke into a raucous laughter as Bill danced away with Alexander's most beloved possession. Hannah bought the glasses two years ago as a Christmas present. Alexander knew she had pawned much of the little jewelry she had to afford it, and he had always treasured them. Soft cases and gentle pockets had thus far kept the heavy frames in one piece, but now they had graced the palms of Sunrise's most destructive student.

A mix of rage and fear exploded in Alexander's eyes as he leapt after the menace, all pain forgotten. April was just getting to her feet, deep hatred carved beneath her eyes, when Alexander shot by her, "accidentally" sending her to the ground for the third time.

"You'll never catch me" Bill laughed coolly. He dived expertly through the rapidly increasing throng of students. Every few moments, the door would open and Bill would have more people to hide behind. He thought Alexander would give up after a few minutes but he pursued his glasses single-mindedly.

"Give it up!" Bill crowed as he ducked past a gaggle of his classmates. The hellion laughed triumphantly in a way that made one think of an evil Peter Pan. But his celebrations were short lived, for at that moment, he began juggling the glasses haphazardly while laughing like a maniac. He had forgotten to watch where he was going and when Alexander leapt at him, quite enraged by now, Bill dove right…and into Molly Hall.

Molly was a legend in her own right. Somewhere beneath her peach-toned oval face, the soft clusters of freckles, and the long and unruly brown hair that framed it all was one of Sunrise's sharpest intellects. Few could hope to equal her impressive feats of academic prowess, from mastering division in mere moments to deciphering the cryptic puzzles they were often given to improve critical thinking. She was usually quiet and often shy but, unlike Alexander, few dared to hassle her very often. Unlike Alexander, Molly understood revenge. When Bill realized whom he had run into, he shook badly, and the glasses flew from his hand.

"Why the hurry?" Molly asked as they skittered across the floor. Alexander shot past the pair and searched the room with his eyes, desperately trying to locate his glasses. But his efforts were suddenly rendered pointless by the sickening crunch of glass ground sadistically beneath a high-top sneaker. The laughter that had permeated the classroom died suddenly. It was replaced by April's triumphant yawp as she continued to stomp the tangled mess beneath her feet.

Molly's normally morose features registered shock at the hateful glee in her classmate's dancing eyes as Alexander folded to the ground like a marionette. Flaring pain returned to lick at his bones and his head felt as if it might explode. A rapidly constricting chest forcefully expelled the air in his lungs but he crawled toward his enemy, determined to cause her an equal amount of pain.

Bill surveyed the chaos he had begun and laughed heartily. Smashing Alexander's glasses had been exactly what he had in mind. Now that April had done it for him, she would be punished and he would be free to plan more chaos.

But Molly had other plans. Her hand flew across Bill's face with the agility and precision of an expertly cracked whip. She followed this with the most effective knee to the stomach he had ever gotten from a little girl in a plain, brown dress. Bill crumpled to the floor as Alexander had, and with a final kick to his legs, Molly dived after Alexander and caught him around his middle.

"Stop struggling!" she said patiently as he tried to shake himself loose from her, "you've been hurt enough today. Trying to fight April won't fix your glasses!" Alexander knew this, but he didn't care. He fought Molly with all the indignation and fury he possessed. For years, April had been asking for the vicious beating he longed to deliver at this moment, and now she would receive it, if Molly would only let him go. But it was useless. The little girl braided her fingers together and dug her feet into the ground. Her face twisted with determination, she tethered Alexander with all her might.

April took full advantage of the situation. Still crushing the broken heap that had once been Alexander's glasses, she

26

called out to him in what she meant to be a sugary voice, but what sounded to Alexander like a mosquito drowning in vinegar.

"Gonna hit me again, Mouse? Or is your little girlfriend going to do it?" At this, laughter crept back into the classroom and Molly's face grew hot and prickly, though whether this was cased by April's remarks or the physical strain of pinning an eight-year-old boy was hard to tell. But before either of them could respond, the door opened once more.

A teacher who genuinely enjoys her work is a very rare thing indeed. Many children will pass through the education system like wayward orphans, without ever having seen one of these marvels. But such a wonder had just stepped foot in Alexander's classroom. Ms. Washington scanned the room expertly. She sported deep forest green eyes that shone like lighthouse beacons upon the slightest sign of trouble. More than a decade of teaching had honed her senses beyond those of what she liked to call the "civilian population". Long, crinkled tresses of soft auburn hair swept behind her as she dashed to the spot where Bill still laid mumbling into the carpet. She was kneeling to help the troublemaker to his feet when she noticed April who, despite having seen her teacher, continued to mash Alexander's glasses defiantly.

Ms. Washington's face, normally a mesmerizing caramel oval, began to fissure with anger. She regained her full height, a feat that never failed to impress, and smoothed the wrinkles in the plain blue dress she was fond of wearing. The laughter she had heard on the way in had stopped short, and when she looked about instinctively, guilty faces were all that greeted her.

"Good morning, class" she began in her usual musically soft voice, "would anyone care to explain what's going on here?" At the sound of her voice, Alexander turned his head so quickly that Molly was thrown off balance, and she fell aside unnoticed. He felt his skin warm as he craned his neck to see her better, and despite all his troubles, he smiled.

Ms. Washington's offer got no takers so she glided elegantly toward April with an inquisitive look on her face, determined to solve the mystery on her own. "Ms. Rainer" she said sweetly as Molly pushed herself into a sitting position, "we do our best to keep this classroom clean. What are you grinding into the carpet?" April was not the least bit afraid of her teacher. In fact, given the circumstances, she was surprised Ms. Washington wasn't terrified of her. Nevertheless, she removed her foot from the shards of glass and twisted metal, laughing wickedly.

"Those were Alexander's glasses. Now they're rubbish." Ms. Washington's voice became even as Molly finally got to her feet, eyes lit with anger.

"And why would you break someone else's property?" the teacher asked, and at that moment a curious thing happened.

April's laughed again but this time it sounded like a soft, sinister whisper. She stepped closer to Ms. Washington and tapped the teacher's nose with an index finger. Alexander had moved into a sitting position behind his teacher, waiting to greet her the moment she finished with April.

"Curiosity killed the cat" April replied in savage undertones, "remember the maid in the garden." Ms. Washington gave her pupil a blank look.

"What on earth is…" But before she could finish, April caught her nose in a heavy pinch. Ms. Washington gritted her teeth against the surprising pain and muttered something in a slightly nasal voice. Alexander didn't hear her the first time, so he cupped his ear as she repeated herself. He distinctly heard his teacher mumble "your little friends don't scare me."

"Class" Ms. Washington began her voice still slightly irregular, "this is the new student I promised the last time we met. Had it not been for certain interruptions" here she glanced sternly at Bill, "we might have had time to let her introduce herself. As things stand, we do not. This is Judith Miller from Washington, DC. Due to a family emergency" a nearly imperceptible scowl crossed her face, "she will be living with me. I hope" she said with conviction, "that she doesn't follow the example of people like Ms. Rainer." She paused for breath. "I would not appreciate having to sentence my niece to a week's detention. With no chance of recess" she finished with emphasis.

The students eyed their new compatriot as she took her seat at the middle octagonal table. Ms. Washington's seating arrangement "coincidentally" placed her between Molly and Alexander, the students least likely to bother her. Normally, April's devilish eyes would be boring through her flesh, looking for weaknesses, but the little troublemaker would spend the rest of the morning in the Principal's office glaring at twisted metal and broken glass.

"Alright class" Ms. Washington began, "this morning, we are going to learn to divide larger numbers." She ignored several rather dramatic groans and continued. "If everyone would kindly open their workbooks, we'll see if we can solve the problems on the board."

Alexander wasn't paying the slightest attention to the problems on the board. His eyes wee locked on his teacher's face and the world around him had ceased to exist. She continued to instruct the class, but all he heard was a sleepy, wafting lullaby. Forgotten were his anger, the pain of April's attacks, and even the loss of his precious glasses. His mind was consumed with the wonder before him and he was suddenly grateful he had not remained at the park.

Beside him, Judith leaned over her workbook, scribbling furiously. Like her aunt, she wore a crown of auburn hair. Her eyes, shielded by a small pair of royal blue box-frames, shone in a lighter, more playful shade of green, like grass on a playground. Her small hand blazed across the page, making notes, working through calculations, but mostly, violently erasing. She began mumbling to herself about columns and places until Molly looked up from her work.

"Calm down" she advised quietly, "or you'll ignite the page. It's only your first day. Besides" she said, leaning over to blow Judith's eraser crumbs away, "if you keep that up you'll never find your work." Judith looked up at Molly and smiled sweetly.

"It doesn't matter" she laughed, "I may never understand how all this works. Move the two, carry the three for goodness' sake am I a student or a juggler?"

Molly giggled loudly, something she rarely did at any volume. At once, several people at the table looked up and Molly dived into her work in case Ms. Washington had heard. She hadn't.

If Molly had glanced at her teacher, she might have noticed that the woman's face was furrowed with thought. A rather thorny problem was weighing on her mind and she was tearing though it for a solution. An hour ago, when April had her by the nose, she had felt indignant and angry. Then she had truly believed that April could not frighten her. Now, surrounded by over two dozen scratching pencils, she wondered how the child's "little friends" would react to their companion's punishment.

Judith noticed that Alexander still hadn't even opened his workbook. She tapped his shoulder several times but Alexander barely noticed. His mind was lying on the cushion of springy grasses Arcadia Park was famous for, offering his bemused teacher Earl Grey in a china cup decorated with violets.

When Molly saw what Judith was up to, she frowned slightly and asked "what are you doing?" in the loudest whisper she could safely muster.

"Well, it's kind of odd he hasn't written anything yet" Judith replied quietly, "and I wanted to ask him about it." Molly sighed heavily as she turned to Alexander, still plainly staring at Ms. Washington, and wondered what he saw in her. She meant to tell Judith to focus on her own work, that what other students did or did not do was none of her concern, but she didn't truly feel that way. Truly, she felt an acute, grasping annoyance she couldn't account for. She skillfully targeted his earlobe with a swift, effective pinch. Seconds later, Alexander was staring dead at her, outrage on every line of his face. For the first time his pencil tore forcefully at the paper before him, and Judith struggled not to laugh.

"He hates when I do that" Molly whispered, satisfied, and without another word, she snatched up her pencil once more. Alexander worked bitterly, robbed of his only peaceful dreams, and when Edwin Cole threw a spitball at him, as he usually did, Alexander reached across the table and jammed the graphite into the back of his classmate's hand.

"Annnnd" Ms. Washington called to her students, "pencils down. Let's see who remembers Friday's lesson. Lucy?" she said, pointing to a short, blond girl with puddles for eyes and a sharp nose, "what did you get for the first problem?"

Somewhere at the third table, the tiny girl shook her head, nodded, looked in every direction, shook her head, wiped her eyes, and answered "six thousand n-n-nine?" in a voice that began as a high squeak and slowly died. Ms. Washington nodded gently and Lucy almost melted from relief.

"Edwin, what's the answer to the second one?" As her aunt continued to quiz the class, Judith's attention began to wane. Out of boredom, she tapped Alexander on his shoulder. On Saturday, when Judith had arrived at her aunt's, a bundle of tears, Ms. Washington had registered her for Sunrise. The thoughtful teacher had also introduced her niece to a fascinating topic: a student incapable of speech. Her interest had been sparked all weekend, and now she intended to witness the spectacle herself. She tapped a second time and Alexander's hand immediately flew to the ear Molly had pinched moments before.

"I'm not gonna pinch you" Judith laughed when Alexander turned to glare darkly at her.

"Yes you will" interjected a dark-skinned boy without looking up from the problems he was checking, "everyone does something to Alexander."

Right on cue, Edwin prepared to fire another spitball but Judith moved her hand to block the projectile's path. "I just want to say hi" she insisted. Alexander waved hello in response, but eyed her suspiciously.

Judith was hurt. She didn't know why but it hurt a lot that Alexander had already taken her for a bully. Perhaps if Ms. Washington had made her niece aware of the sheer volume of bullies at Sunrise, she might have felt better. As it was Judith felt she had been done an injustice and resolved to prove herself unworthy of the title.

"Jonathan" Ms. Washington called, but before she could ask, the dark-skinned boy called out, "three hundred seventy times one hundred twenty equals forty four thousand four hundred."

"Is he right Alexander?" Judith asked, hoping for some response. Alexander looked up at her, surprised, and nodded. He pointed to the number, engraved halfway down his workbook page, and began to turn away from her. Judith sighed.

"You'd think I was poison" she grumbled audibly. Molly uttered something unintelligible in reply.

"You're gonna pinch him aren't you?" Jonathan asked knowingly. In a huff, Judith punched him in the arm.

"You were what?" the shadow asked coldly, glaring from its side of the table. It was lunchtime at Sunrise and, since no punishment devised by the school could legally prevent it, April had rejoined her compatriots in the All-Purpose Room. The room was just a massive area of space that, as the name stated, could be used for whatever purpose the principal dreamed up. When it was used as the school cafeteria, it featured row upon row of cold, splintery, white picnic tables, and two streams of red tape on the stained marble floor clearly marking the line for food. April sat before one of the uncomfortable tables and quivered noticeably. Her expression, normally featuring a fierce cunning, was now pale, devoid of the faintest sign of courage.

Though the room was brightly lit by clusters of fluorescent lights, she faced what was undeniably a veil of darkness. It was a grim and imposing shadow, and it belonged to a peculiarly dark-hearted little girl.

Helen Greywiche had arrived at Sunrise about three years ago, a morose, silent, antisocial individual. Since then, a collection of morbid and sinister rumors accompanied her rise to prominence among Sunrise's troubled students. As she sat before this awful figure, April could not help recalling these frightful whispers, and soon her eyes were widening in sheer terror.

Helen glared at the bundle of nerves across from her and laughed dryly.

"I have warned you before to carry out your assignments with more stealth." She leaned over slowly, her darting red eyes burning like hot coals, "now you will just have to convince her otherwise." Helen caught the front of April's shirt in one of her chalk-white hands. "You serve no purpose in detention" she growled quietly, "do you understand?"

At her final word, Helen traced one of her fingernails along April's throat. At once, her world disappeared, replaced by her own deafening screams. April felt blood run down her neck in rivers but passers-by saw and heard nothing but two girls having a conversation. Artic winds tore at April's skin and she felt the table beneath her crumble into dust. Her hands shot out, instinctively trying to find something to hold on to.

"LILITH!" she yelled at the top of her lungs, and her tormentor, still gripping April's shirt, replied with a cold laugh. Darkness enveloped the spirit that had burned so brightly that morning.

No one wondered what April was yelling about, for none heard her cries. From where Molly sat, eyeing her with unbridled hatred, the girl was simply having a chat, although she shook a little more than usual. Molly turned back to the mysterious, unappetizing dish the school had provided for her. It had looked like an egg roll when it was placed in her tray, but when she cut it open using the badly designed "spork" she had been given, she found it contained grayish tuna slathered with American cheese. She wasn't interested. Sighing, she looked up from her tray, meaning to ask Alexander for something from the lunch he always brought from home. But Alexander was not in his usual seat, across from her. Instead she met a pair of playful green eyes.

Judith wasn't eating. She had been scrawling something on a piece of paper, and she folded it into a neat square and slid it to her right. Alexander feigned disinterest in the offering until Judith moved to slide it closer. At once, Alexander deftly swept up the note, moving his ear out of her reach.

"Ugh!" Judith groaned, frustrated, "she pinched you, not me." And for effect, she pointed dramatically at Molly. Ignoring her, Molly turned in her seat to face Alexander.

"She" Molly said, mimicking Judith's tone, "saved you from turning in nothing this morning and thinks half a sandwich is a good reward." At the mention of the morning's work Alexander turned away to hide a hot blush. He was certain Molly had seen where he'd been looking and he quickly divided his sandwich, hoping to change the subject.

"How come he listens to you?" Judith asked, her note still unopened. Here she had gone to all the trouble of thinking of a way they could "talk" and he was still trying to brush her off. Judith wondered why it even mattered to her. Usually when people were rude, Judith was adept at telling them so, and leaving. This time though, she couldn't convince herself to just walk away. And it was beginning to bother her.

Nearby, somewhere on her left, came a lazy yawn of a reply.

"He listens to her cause she's the only one who'll go near him. Can't stand the smell myself." All three looked up and saw Bill Wildre lazily munching a candy apple. At once, Alexander snatched up Judith's note and for one awful moment, she was afraid he'd rip it in twain. But he threw it down at the last second and fished out the rumpled notepad he had used that morning. His hand raced across the small page with blinding speed before tearing out the sheet and handing it to Judith. She had to squint to read the messy scrawl but when she made it out, a smile crossed her lips.

She handed the slip of paper to Bill who, after greedily devouring the remaining apple, dramatically covered his hand with his sleeve before accepting it.

"And just what color were those sleeves when you bought them?" Molly interjected. Bill gave one sleeve a fleeting glance and returned to his note. Molly looked smug. When he had purchased the shirt about a week ago the sleeves had been off-white. Now they were a dingy gray and covered in small black balls of lint.

Bill had no trouble reading the single word printed in the center: INVICTUS.

"What's in-vyct-hus?" he asked the room.

"Give me that!" Molly cried, and snatched the note in exasperation. "It's Latin" she remarked after a moment. "It means "unconquered". Her eyes caught the words that had made Judith smile. "Good morning" was wedged in a corner of the sheet. Molly sighed. Alexander was tired of being lonely.

"Some are born for recess, some achieve recess and some have recess thrust upon them" Amelia Dickinson stood atop of the "twisty slide" shouting her wisdom like a forgotten queen. Most of it was sound and fury, signifying boredom. When her hair wasn't whipping across her eyes, she could see Alvin Eldridge leading a pack of unidentifiable classmates in an out of a football shaped jungle gym. Behind her, children scuttled nimbly up cargo nets, spun down sliding poles, and swung across the monkey bars, completely contented with their limited freedom. Halfway across the oft-trampled grasses that made up Sunrise's playground a lazy game of soccer was coming to an end. A rotund, hoary and liver spotted bald man ran amongst the students shouting out directions. Despite his appearance Coach McGregor was a formidable athlete, something he demonstrated with a fierce kick of the soccer ball in mid run.

"That", he cried as the sphere appeared to sail into the clouds, "is what a real kick looks like!"

Beyond the field, at the playground's furthest edge there stood a massive creation that was called a tree simply because no other term would adequately describe it. At least forty tall, it towered into the clear, blue, sky. Yet unlike most trees, its branches spread out, like an overlarge bush, and draped down, concealing the first two thirds of the trunk. The last third was sealed from view by an overgrowth of brambles and thorny bushes that skirted the tree like the moats that safeguarded old English castles. These plants had yet to yield to pruning of any sort and their wild strength had been the death of several saws and other cutting tools. It was here, in this natural fort, that Alexander now lay reclined. High in its branches he gazed at what little sky could be seen through the wall of leaves, and pondered Judith's note.

He had been fascinated with the impossibly beautiful tree since his arrival at Sunrise but it had taken a month of recesses to discover an entrance through the curtain of thorny branches woven into the fence that marked the playground's end. On that day, he carefully stepped into the dark world he called "Cradle", and had hidden there ever since. He squinted to see a few defiant beams of sunlight penetrate the thick canopy. This forced his missing glasses back into his mind, but no anger came with the bitter recollection. Cradle was a safe haven, another realm in which there were no dire dreams, horrid visions or heartless foes. There was only semi-darkness and cool shade. It seemed as if Nature itself would not permit his rage, so the thought merely swirled lazily in his mind, like an autumn leaf caught in a wind.

"Besides", some inner voice counseled, "there are more important thoughts." *Like the words in her note*. Judith had made a request Alexander had never seen in writing before. In fact, he had never heard it spoken either. Not even Molly had made such an offer, though she, unlike many, could often be found near him. In simple but neat manuscript, the note read "I want to be your friend."

Below this was a surprisingly well done sketch of the benches on the blacktop near the school's side entrance. One of them was normally occupied by Emma Prescott, a bespectacled young teaching assistant, but the drawing showed Judith sitting alone, patiently waiting.

Could he trust her? A similar situation had occurred only a year ago. An innocent looking fourth grader named Ellen had promised him a kiss if he would only follow her to the edge of the park once school ended. Alexander had been certain something terrible would happen but curiosity had driven him to go anyway. He had hoped this "Ellen" person would become his friend, and give him the kind of protection only a fourth grader could provide, but instead...

Still, his home was a lonely place where few people could stand him, as was his school, and Alexander was tired of solitude. Even the slimmest chance that he might one day have a friend who would call him so in broad daylight had to be taken. He slid to the ground with practiced ease and stepped beyond his Cradle, wincing as the full sunlight hammered his eyes.

He hadn't taken twelve steps when a blood chilling scream rang across the playground. Several heads turned as the horrible cry resounded and a few had located its source. Alexander rarely ran. Even when faced with a hail of small stones Alexander had merely quickened his pace. But at this moment he launched himself toward the blacktop with the force of a cannon. His sprints became a series of leaps and turns over and around all that crossed his path. In his mind, Ms. Washington's words echoed uncertainly: "your little friends don't scare me."

By the time he reached it, the blacktop was enfolded in a ring of curious students. The screams were louder now, mercilessly spearing his eardrums, and at last, Ms. Prescott was coming to investigate, clutching a thin romance novel. Alexander shoved madly through the crowd, struggling against arms that meant to block his progress, and legs that thought to imperil his health. Finally, he emerged and beheld, in the ring's center, the only person ever to ask for his friendship. Judith Miller writhed on the ground shrieking in pain every few seconds. Both her eyes had been blackened by violence, and her nose ran with blood. Her glasses were furrowed with cracks and fractures and had been tossed several feet away. Some of her hair had been cut away viciously, and wisps of it clung to the sturdy brown dress she wore, which despite their location was marred with streaks of dirt. Tears streamed from sickly purple veils as Alexander finally reached her. He took her in his arms, tears and blood, cascading down his shirt, and tried to say something comforting. Instantly, his throat was on fire and he clamped his mouth shut so fast he savagely bit his lip.

Alexander couldn't understand how his classmates could watch someone do this without interfering. How could anyone be so callous and hateful as to allow this to happen? But at that moment, Judith's eyes widened in recognition, and she forced herself to compose enough breath for one last word: "April".

"I know how you must feel Aries, but what you suggest solves nothing." Vice Principal Allen Bellerose sat behind the rickety, wooden desk of his cluttered office. For the last ten minutes he had been sitting amidst a scattering of announcements, report cards, records and appointment notices listening to the rantings of his least favorite employee. Usually reserved and quiet, Ms. Washington had gone ballistic when Alexander ran into the Teacher's Lounge and dragged her to Judith. Besides the scrapes and bruises Alexander had noted, both of Judith's legs were discovered to be broken. Ms. Prescott had summoned an ambulance but she wasn't of much further help as all she had to offer was her story of a few scattered screams. Aries had thoroughly chewed her out for failing to be an effective playground monitor, but Emma stood beside her, nonplused, as Aries demanded action.

"How can you know how I feel?" she asked hotly. "Is a niece of yours in a hospital with her nose and legs broken? Did her parents die right in front of her just a few days ago? She's hospitalized on her first day here because this incompetent" here she jabbed her finger at Ms. Prescott, "could not do her job and now you tell me punishing the girl who did this would "solve nothing"?"

Bellerose sighed. A diminutive and thin man whose short, frayed, black hair had begun to show flecks of gray, Allen Bellerose was always known to be tired. When he arrived for work each morning, it was with a drooping sort of gait that the strongest pots of coffee had failed to remedy. He feared disruption above all else and it was this trait that fueled his dislike of Ms. Washington. As her request wafted through his mind like an errant wind, he sighed more deeply.

"Look, Aries, I cannot expel the child just because she upset you this morning. You say she threatened you but there's no proof." He waved away a budding protest. "You do not offer a single witness to corroborate the claim. So what am I to offer against her when she denies it?" Ms. Washington opened her mouth again but was once more waved into silence. "Further you suspended her recess privileges for the remainder of the week if I am not mistaken. I told you this morning that such a punishment is far to harsh, especially since it comes with a week's detention."

"She broke a student's glasses!" Ms. Washington cut in lividly. "Those things cost hundreds of dollars. She threatened me when I asked her about it, and one student says April hit one of her classmates. For no reason."

"At least ten students say Ms. Hall made that up" Bellerose countered in a low simmer, "and as I've said before, I have no proof she made any such threat. All I have in evidence is a pair of broken glasses, and even those prove nothing. She claims it was an accident. My original point" Bellerose rushed to cut off more debate, "was that Ms. Rainer was in the detention area during the recess period. Mrs. Chandler confirms this. So how can Ms. Rainer be responsible when she was inside the entire time?"

Ms. Washington had no answer for this but she wasn't backing down yet. The smug look plastered across Ms. Prescott's face was beginning to boil the blood of the intrepid educator.

"My niece said April attacked her. Alexander told me so when he came to get me. As you know, he is one of the school's best students. I find it hard to believe he made that up."

"I don't" Ms. Prescott chimed in suddenly, and Ms. Washington glared. Emma had spent three years working for Sunrise as a substitute teacher and playground monitor. Both jobs were, in her estimation, relatively easy, requiring her to look in on her charges every now and then, something like a preoccupied babysitter. Yet whenever Alexander joined the ranks of her charges, she found her novels interrupted far more often, and by now she had come to dread his constant complaints against his classmates. These days, she would find it easy to believe anything of the child that featured prominently in her after-hours conversation as "that spoiled brat at work."

But Bellerose concurred. "I don't see how the concept's hard to grasp" he intoned slowly, as if addressing a remedial pupil, "my guess would be that Mr. Lightarrow sought to punish Ms. Rainer for the destruction of his glasses. Accidental or otherwise. As I have noted previously there is no evidence to place the child at the scene."

"The children nearby?" Ms. Washington asked, quivering with impotent frustration.

"Saw nothing!" came Prescott's swift reply.

"And what about you?" Ms. Washington indicated Emma accusingly, "they were a few feet away. Don't tell me you didn't see anything". At once, Prescott replied evenly.

"Obviously, the fight started at the other end of the playground. Your girl's dress was covered in dirt after all. I responded as soon as I saw the problem but I cannot always prevent these things from happening." By now, Aries was beyond reasonable, calm debate. She exploded with rage, grabbing the front of her colleague's dress.

"You're telling me" she bellowed savagely, "that someone can get two black eyes, a broken nose and" she paused for emphasis "two broken legs before you notice something's wrong?" "Answer me!" she screamed madly as she shook Ms. Prescott like a rag doll.

Bellerose slowly rose to restrain Ms. Washington but Emma neither struggled nor lost the smug expression on her face. Instead, she simply pulled back the left sleeve of her light, beige, cotton sweater to reveal the underside of her wrist. When Aries saw that bit of flesh she released her colleague at once, a quizzical look etched in her face. There, just below the joint, was a bold Celtic spiral the color of blood.

The second classroom on the left of Sunrise's third floor emptied slowly as the school day drew to a close. By now, word of Judith's "mishap" had reached every classroom and play area. It was unlike Aries to sit lethargically in her rocking chair as her students filed out unsupervised, but the sight of Emma's spiral tore at her mind. The symbol was familiar enough to her by now. Several of the school's more problematic bullies proudly displayed the emblem. Until a year ago, she had believed the sign to be the invention of the most frequent occupants of detention. She thought of it only as a poor attempt to look "cool".

Then one day, April began to display the spiral and things changed. Instead of irreverent disrespect for the rules, those who wore the brand began to work toward organized action. In the beginning, few noticed the change, and the new group developed a reputation among Sunrise's revenant population for escaping punishment regardless of the offense. Ms. Washington began to pay them more attention then, especially when they began to occasionally vandalize some of the quieter teachers' belongings. Yet no one else seemed to notice the trend, and now, she knew why.

What she couldn't understand was what a teacher could possibly gain by helping a group of bullies. She was certain now that Ms. Prescott had allowed Judith to be attacked, but she could not wrap her mind around the reasoning behind it. They couldn't possibly be paying her, after all, because they were children, and for the same reason it was unlikely that they had intimidated her. Ms. Washington tried to remember her colleague's expressions: calm, smug, nonplussed. Why wasn't she worried for her job? Why had she shown her the spiral? Surely she didn't think children could provide her adequate job security?

Lost to these thoughts, Ms. Washington failed to realize she was not alone. Though class had been dismissed some time ago, Alexander sat in his assigned place gazing at a crumpled sheet of white paper, and crying softly. He was convinced that if he had read the note earlier, he might have arrived to the blacktop in time to spare Judith some of her pan. His insides felt painfully tangled as his tears stained much of Judith's picture.

That moment, a brutal-sounding crash brought Aires back to the present.

"What in the name of…" she began, but she caught sight of Alexander as she turned toward the noise. "Alexander?" she asked, surprised, "what are you doing here? School ended some time ago. And what's the matter?" she asked, wiping his eyes with a napkin she produced from a pocket as if by magic, "Judith will be fine, I promise."

But Alexander just pointed at the scrap of paper like a stubborn two year old, weeping quietly. Curious, Aries smoothed the paper as flat as she could get it, and among several dark patches she could just make out Judith's drawing. Her eyes lit up.

"When did she give this to you?"

She had evidence. It was flimsy, she knew, but it meant something. It meant that Judith was on the blacktop, had been on Emma's bench, and had planned on staying there until Alexander showed up. It wasn't enough to contradict the information Bellerose now possessed, but Ms. Prescott would have to explain it, and maybe then she'd let something slip.

Ms. Washington had walked about a third of the twelve or so blocks to the Salvere Hospital with these thoughts buzzing in her mind. She barely felt the tug of Alexander's hand in hers as they marched through what was increasingly becoming a narrow strip of sidewalk. Beside them, the stores and apartments had given way to more forest bordered by a metal barrier that made one think of a fat man wearing an undersized belt.

It had taken a lot of paper, but Alexander had finally explained his guilty feelings, and Aires had assured him that he wasn't to blame. To make sure he felt better, and because his mother worked there, according to Alexander, she had invited him to the hospital to visit Judith. Instantly, Alexander's tears had vanished and the child became all smiles and nods.

All the way to her car, she had been thinking that Alexander looked a little too happy all of a sudden. For some time, she had been well aware of Alexander's feelings for her. Indeed, her exploitation of them had forged him into a model student. Straight as an arrow and smart as a whip, Alexander would do anything to impress his teacher.

Aires felt guilty about that. She was supposed to have sat him down for a long, uncomfortable conversation ages ago, but she kept putting it off to spare the child's feelings. She had met him in kindergarten, and every bit of his life she had seen was filled with misery. She had finally convinced herself of the necessity of the lecture when Alexander stopped talking, and that just broke her heart. So she had silenced herself once more, and hoped he'd grow out of it.

She had arrived at the faculty parking lot to discover her tires slashed. Craterous holes pockmarked what remained of the windshield. The windows were now so many shards of glass strewn across the salt and pepper, cloth covered seats, and a spiral was scratched into the paint. Deep. So she and Alexander were walking, and tomorrow, someone would answer for that as well.

Aires turned from her thoughts when her hand began to feel lighter than it should. Sure enough, it was empty, and she looked about frantically for Alexander. She found him a few feet ahead perched on the border rail and watching her intently. She sighed,

"I'll straighten him out as soon as this is over" she promised herself, "Alexander, please stay nearby. Think of this as a field trip." A moment later Alexander fell in near-military step behind her, his eyes wide with admiration.

At length the empty street turned into the sprawling parking lot of the massive hospital and Aries led her charge through the sliding doors of the emergency room. Moments later they stood before room 218 which was said to contain one Judith Miller.

"But this is madness" a worn voice sighed desperately, "your little pranks are one thing, but this will bring the police again. Have you any idea how hard it is to keep fooling...."

Before the Vice Principal could finish, the joint of his left wrist began to swell painfully. As Bellerose's face began to pinch with agony, a cold voice replied him from a shaded corner of his office.

"I visited Miriam's finest during the previous incident" it spat harshly, "they won't return." Bellerose shook nervously in his seat. This was not going well.

"Look" he tried again, "Aires is going to ask about her car. She'll want to investigate. She could sue the school over her niece's injuries. You have to stop doing thisaaaaaaaaaaggggggghhhh."

His wrist seemed to explode with inhuman waves of pain. Blood fell from the tri-spiral etched there in heavy droplets. Helen stepped out of the shadows, absently sweeping shocks of rust-toned hair from her eyes. Pale and fiercely beautiful, she advanced toward the principal who began frantically struggling

44

to back away in his chair. In his haste, he pushed to hard and fell to the floor, banging his toe on the way down. Helen stood above him and laughed pitilessly.

"I don't have to do anything" she replied amid his screams, "but lure Alexander to our side. By striking her niece, I have removed his only friend and shown all before me the price of my displeasure. If I had allowed April's punishment unchallenged, the others would doubt me" she swooped down and caught his broken wrist, "as you do" she finished, and began to trace his spiral. Instantly, the blood receded and the pain dimmed. Bellerose's screams turned to whimpers and Helen's face broke into a terrifying expression that combined a sneer and a smirk.

"She will neither sue nor investigate. She lacks the money for one and the time for the other. When I am finished, she will simply be happy she's alive and keep her mouth shut. Just like you." A flash of thought filled Bellerose's mind with an image of his furrowed hands holding down a pillow with force.

"You swore never to mention that!" he cried fearfully.

"And you swore to obey without question" she reminded him carelessly. "You might have found a better hiding pace than a dumpster though" she added cruelly, and Bellerose erupted with tears that had nothing to do with pain. "The point is" she continued, ignoring him, "I will not change my plan. You will put my Grigori where they may do their work. " Still in tears, the old man nodded.

"And Amanda?" he asked, referring to Sunrise's principal.

"Claim her loyalty!" Helen ordered in reply.

Judith was tucked in a hospital bed that was shielded by a curtain from another patient whose ailment was unknown. Her nose continued to bleed, though not as badly as before, and twin casts suspended her pencil-thin legs. Some sort of salve coated her eyes, which showed signs of healing, though they had become puffy from a long crying session. The nurse was just finishing up with her thermometer when Ms. Washington arrived.

"Well, now!" the frizzy-haired nurse cried cheerfully, "looks like you've got visitors Judith." Aires ran to her niece, trailed by Alexander, and gave the child a gentle hug.

"Are you alright? Do you feel okay? Does it hurt?" Judith nodded as her aunt peppered her with questions, until the nurse caught her shoulder and whispered in her ear.

"I'm glad you brought Alexander." she shook her head sadly, "because Judith shows all of his symptoms. Including loss of voice." Ms. Washington looked at her niece, then back at the nurse, her expression instantly lost to desperation "H..h..ow did this..." She was seized by a fit of tears before she could finish. The nurse caught Aires in a consoling hug and explained slowly, trying to master the chipper notes that naturally filled her voice.

"We can't tell what's the matter with her yet. Alexander is the only other case of something like this on record so we went through all his tests. All we've managed to find is a strange looking spiral on her thigh."

At once, Ms. Washington was alert. So far, she'd seen spirals on Emma and her car. She also knew April wore one. And now Judith had one just when her voice had vanished.

"Alexander!" she cried suddenly, and the child leapt to attention at once. He'd been playing the walk to the hospital in his mind as a continuous loop. The nurse asked whether he had a spiral on his body, explaining that Judith did, and was showing his symptoms. When he shrugged to indicate he didn't know, she called over an aide and chortled "let's find out".

Aires' niece fell into a fit of silent giggles as Alexander attempted to elude capture. Ordinarily, Alexander had an extreme dislike for hospitals. Whether it was the long hours in the waiting room, the shots or trading in his clothes for a flimsy hospital gown, he hated the experience and did all he could to avoid it. He had agreed this time to see Judith, and because Aires was taking him. He had never gotten an opportunity to be alone with his teacher until today. But he wasn't going to allow himself

46

to be searched for spirals. Not again. He figured the medical staff at this hospital had seen enough of him already.

Aires couldn't believe her eyes. Her normally slow-paced, and obedient pupil was darting between legs and around tables with uncharacteristic dexterity and speed.

"Calm down, Alexander!" she called unhelpfully, but not even Ms. Washington's voice could tame him now.

"If ya catchim lemme beat im firs" came a raspy voice from beyond the curtain, and when Alexander recognized it as belonging to Dottie Jenkins, he dived for the doorway.

He might have escaped were it not for a bit of cleverness from Aires. Sure, she felt guilty about doing it but she needed any information that would help her niece. So she called out to the nurse "He'll stop if you promise to kiss him!" Just seconds away from freedom, he turned beet red, fueling Judith's silent giggles, and collided with the wall next to the door. He was immediately caught by the cheerful nurse who now looked like the victor of a spirited game of freeze tag.

"Nice work, Nancy" laughed the approaching aide, and as he dragged Alexander away to be examined in private, Aires clearly saw an accusatory look on his face.

Judith finally quieted down and her aunt sat beside her to await the nurse's findings. The only sounds in the room now were a boring rerun on the small television overhead, and the expletive-ridden ranting of the room's other occupant. Apparently, she had once again missed out on a chance to punish the boy whose screams interrupted her sleep.

Aires wondered if her niece would greet each morning the way Dottie insisted Alexander did, whether she would ever be normal again.

"This is the worst time for this" she thought to herself, "after her parents...."

Judith's parents had been lawyers for a civil rights organization in Washington known as The Starlight Institute. Named for a community outreach program founded by Daniel Rivulet a wealthy child with a stunning intellect, the

Institute collected research from around the country and used it to support their various legal battles. Alvin and Leah Miller were working on strengthening legislation associated with hate crimes and it had won them many enemies. One in particular, Prescott Reaver, seemed to believe that their efforts hurt the cause by allowing what he called "a few trivial happenings" to consume the energy of the movement. That was still his position when, a few days ago, masked figures had charged the Miller residence in broad daylight and fired assault weapons through the first floor windows. Judith had survived only by diving under the wide living room sofa. And so, social workers had delivered the girl into her aunt's temporary custody. And now she was hospitalized.

Judith suddenly tapped her aunt's shoulder.

"Yes?" Aires asked, turning to her niece. The child mimed pouring something into a cup, and pointed to the nightstand slightly beyond her reach.

Just as Aires rose to fetch her niece a glass of water, the doors to 218 opened to reveal the nurse, her aide, and Alexander, whose face radiated pure, seething anger.

"It couldn't have been that bad" Aires commented as she handed Judith the glass, "could it?" In response, he turned away from her for the first time since they had met. Aries' face registered shock. Shaking of the nurse's attempts at consolation, he folded his arms, shut his eyes and lowered his head. When repeated attempts to talk to him failed, Aires turned her attention to the nurse.

"Did you find anything?" she asked hopefully. Nurse Collins nodded.

"My assistant Erwin tells me the kid has a spiral at the base of his spine that is identical to the one I found on your niece's thigh. Unfortunately, this means you can expect her to face sleepless nights, a lot of screaming and severe pain any time she attempts to speak. I'm sorry but there's nothing we can do about it." Alexander nearly ripped his right pocket off as he dug out his notepad. He wrote furiously, then handed his work to

Judith. In bold, angry letters it read "stay awake!"

Chapter Two: Antebellum

The following morning was full of surprises; chief among them, was that Judith returned to school. Aires had argued against it all night and into the morning, but her niece insisted on attending. And so she now sat just as before between Molly and Alexander, in a squeaky wheelchair, absently rubbing her still swollen eyes.

Alexander was even more upset now than he had been last night. He felt betrayed by the teacher he had always loved. She had deliberately stopped him long enough to be caught and subjected to a humiliating inspection. When they discovered the spiral, they conducted a series of tests, each more uncomfortable than the last, during which time, the truth had dawned on him. He realized now that his teacher was using his feelings for her to extract obedience, and he despised himself for not recognizing it thus far. All morning he had been stubborn, unresponsive and flippant, and Aires wasn't taking it well.

It hadn't helped that Molly, true to form, had exacted revenge on Bill and April by planting baking soda volcanoes in their cubbies. The two bullies had arrived to find their possessions covered in thick foam or soaked through beyond all hope of rescue. The ensuing chaos took thirty minutes to calm down.

By lunchtime, Aires had never been more exhausted in her life. She just couldn't believe how wild things had become. Sighing deeply, she snatched up her aching frame and slowly marched toward the Teacher's Lounge to unveil a surprise of her own. Pondering the many spirals she had seen, and their connection to Judith's welfare had kept Aires up long after her niece had fallen into a fitful sleep. This had been just as well because shortly afterward, her phone began ringing incessantly.

Apparently, nearly three-fourths of Sunrise's third grade parents had learned of Judith's injuries through the eager reports of their children. Now they wanted to know what was being done to safeguard them, and after the ninth or tenth call, she had called an emergency PTA meeting to be held at noon the following morning. Something she was discovering she didn't have the authority to do.

"Further" opined an especially weary looking Bellerose, "dragging the parents out here using scare tactics and half-truths is irresponsible and unethical. Now" he intoned, cutting Aires off, "you've brought us all here to persecute a little girl out of irrational sympathy, our actions justified by the flimsiest evidence. Is that right? Well, let's have it."

Aires made to reply, but a rotund, pale-faced woman with short, scattered red curls spoke up in a wheezing sort of growl.

"We're here to learn" she gasped with difficulty, "how a kid gets er legs broke in front of the monitor. So how bout it?" Without missing a beat, Bellerose gave a frustrated sigh.

"You have your facts wrong Mrs. Covington" he spoke wearily, "despite what this teacher may have told you, when we last discussed this matter we agreed the evidence indicated that the girl was at the far end of the playground when the attack occurred. This sensationalizing of..."

Bellerose was halted in mid-sentence when Aires, by this time forcefully gritting her teeth, shoved Judith's note in his face.

"This was drawn by Judith at lunchtime on the day of the attack and given to Alexander. It indicates that she planned to wait for him on the monitor's bench on the blacktop for the entire recess period if necessary. This is proof she was almost beside the monitor the entire time!"

With a hateful glare, Bellerose snatched up the note, nearly tearing it, and examined it closely, amid the mummers of an increasing number of the parents in attendance. At length, the vice-principal looked up from the scrap of paper and proclaimed.

"Will Alexander testify to any of this foolishness?" When Aires faltered slightly, Bellerose's lips split into a badly hidden "smile" resembling a jagged streak of lightning.

Alexander had spent the morning exhibiting behaviors no one had seen in him before. Aires had arrived to find her chalk missing, and various board games strewn across the floor. She was just about to punish Bill Wildre out of habit when she spotted Alexander hurling chalk out of an open window on the far side of the room. His face boiling with rage, he glared coldly at her as he tossed out the remnant. She tried to talk to him but he simply held up his hand to demand silence, and marched to his assigned seat, trampling several board games along the way.

Later, she was shocked to discover that, rather than the brilliant ideas that usually filled his workbook, Alexander had chosen to draw and color various animals including a crocodile the color of split-pea soup. But it was the captions that raised her ire, for they titled the series "Things My Teacher Is Uglier Than: Part One". For the first time, he was sentenced to detention.

But things had only gotten worse. As usual, Edwin peppered him with spitballs, laughing as each soggy bullet found its mark. But Molly and Judith were horribly astonished to see Alexander take aim and fire a similar device at their teacher. Ever the snitch, Edwin called out "Duck!" and Ms. Washington turned in time to catch a stellar blow to the eye. As she remembered this, Aires felt her blood steaming inside her. How dare he treat her this way. After all, he was her prize student. She had molded him into a perfect pupil and given him every opportunity to succeed. Why should he make such a fuss over a few harmless tests that would improve the lives of his only friends?

"Yes!" she answered forcefully. "Both Alexander and Judith will support this evidence". Still smiling, Bellerose stood slowly as if he were an ancient skeleton, and leisurely crossed to the front of his desk. Ever since his conversation with Helen, he'd become much more motivated to perform his job correctly.

Rearranging his face to reflect an air of the patient elder, he addressed the parents.

"Sunrise" he began slowly, "is, has and always will be a safe learning environment. One of our children is guilty of bringing harm to this woman's niece, and understandably, she wants justice done. We are doing all we can to achieve that goal, including interviewing the relevant parties, gathering credible evidence, and appointing additional monitors to cover a wider area of the playground. As well, the school counselor will visit each classroom to explain alternate methods of conflict resolution to the students. But unfounded speculation hampers these efforts. I have discussed the matter with the principal, the relevant monitor, and Mrs. Chandler, who is in charge of our detention system. They agree on two things: that this event will not be repeated, and that the girl you were called here to punish..."

He was suddenly interrupted by the booming, kingly voice of Mr. C. J. Roberts III, Jonathan's father. "We were not called here" he intoned heavily, "we phoned Ms. Washington when our children told us thy saw the fight." Aires' ears perked up immediately.

If Ms. Washington's class had been unmanageable in their classroom, the freedom offered by recess drove them wild. Amelia's proclamations were especially random today and many below actually gazed at her in confusion. Jonathan tore through the soccer field like a force of nature, sending clouds of dust and grass flying around him. Angela Edwards had organized a game of double dutch that had devolved into a disorderly mess, and, near the fence at the playground's end, April was having an animated conversation with a gaggle of her peers. She was freed from her teacher's punishments by order of the Vice Principal, an order, Helen was sure, Aires would fail to challenge. Once again at liberty, she was searching for a way to stay on what little good side Helen had.

"S..so what are we d…doing today?" asked a shaky, whimpering voice.

"*We* aren't doing anything" April replied briskly, "you're still in the first Order. Those of us who don't need more training will be shadowing our target."

"Alexander?" another voice piped up excitedly.

"Yes you nitwit!" was April's reply. "Lilith has driven away his loyalty to our nuisance of a teacher, I have kept the teacher's niece away from him, and everyone but Lucy" here she indicated the tiny girl who was still whimpering to herself, "has made his life miserable. At every misfortune he has suffered there has been a spiral, and his curiosity must be growing. If we work at it, he may join us today. Today!" she repeated with emphasis. "A year's worth of effort could finally yield results before school ends. Alvin will take two people from the second Order and make sure that happens" she finished.

Alvin Eldridge swept a hand confidently through his dingy, brown hair. Under the shade of a nearby tree, he looked pale and rat-like.

"You and you" he ordered shortly, pointing at two girls. A moment later, the trio broke away from the group.

"Now then " April began again, watching them go, "I want three volunteers to find Molly Robin Hall and punish her. Severely." April didn't particularly care for any of the schoolbooks and other belongings she had found drenched in foam. She did, however, mind being a laughingstock before her classmates, and her terror at the punishment Helen had delivered had long become a cool anger.

But the assignment had few takers. No one wanted to attack anyone else. They feared it would be an admission of guilt for all the mischief the previous day had held. Worse, no one wanted to cross Molly, who could express her anger in ways far more dangerous than an overflow of foam. At length, April sneered.

"No volunteers, huh? Alright. Then I'll force someone." She thought for a moment then indicated Emily Archer, a caramel-colored wild child in braces.

"You and Wild Bill here will raid her cubby for everything its worth while she's in Social Studies. Not a word!" she added when Emily opened her mouth to protest. "Get to it!" she yelled forcefully, and the pair scattered.

"A...and me?" Lucy asked timidly. She was the only person remaining. April briskly replied, "come with me".

As predicted, Alexander had indeed grown curious about the spirals. Indeed, the longing to understand his dreams was all that brought him to school that morning. They began the previous night exactly as always, roiling with terror and blind fear, except that this time, as he gazed upon the crimson spirals, he saw the girl. Blue dress, graying skin, covered in gashes.

Alexander's screams were nothing to her own. All night she shrieked on an on, chilling his soul to the point where he tore at his ears for relief. Just before his guardian woke him, the flesh began to color, the eyes melted into green pools and the gashes mended. When his eyes shot open that morning he uttered a new word for the first time in a year.

"Judith".

He'd been bitter all morning. The more he considered the spirals, the angrier he became. His teacher crept into his mind, and the rage grew hotter still. Some part of him screamed that her offense was trivial, but it was drowned instantly in waves of memory. As the pain and humiliation of the tests came to mind, he grew spiteful, beginning to feel true hatred for the first time.

By lunchtime he couldn't look at Judith or her aunt without wanting to hurt them. Somehow, he thought, they were the cause of his pain.

He joined his classmates on the playground with one goal in mind: to find the person he hated most in the world, and his only link to the spirals. He planned to climb the twisty slide in order to search the playground from a high vantage point but such plans were rendered unnecessary when his arms were suddenly seized.

"Hello again!" cried a mocking voice, and they dragged him toward the shade.

"Do you know why you're here?" Alvin asked again. Alexander wasn't listening. His eyes focused on the girl behind Alvin's right shoulder, the source of the voice that had called to him.

"I see you remember me" she laughed, brushing away several strawberry blond tresses, "I didn't think anyone could defy Lilith and live".

Alvin turned to glance interestingly at her. Placing his hand thoughtfully on his chin, he considered his compatriot with a bemused smile.

"Ah, so you're the miserable failure." He laughed darkly, "you let him go!" The girl stared at Alvin with hate-filled blue eyes.

"We'll resolve that today!" she shouted, though uncertainty flashed over her face.

That moment Alexander struggled free of his captors only to be caught once more by the girl on Alvin's right.

"I mean it" she cried fiercely. Laughing scornfully, Alvin continued his speech.

"About a year ago", he began arrogantly, "you were Elected. Our mistress asked some of us to lure you to her so we had Ellen here trick you. She drew you in, I forget how, and left you to your conversion. But somehow" here he glanced to his right, "you failed to join us. Your suffering is a result of that."

Ellen laughed as Alexander pulled one of his arms from her grip. Pointing at her he screamed something fiercely. Instantly, his eyes watered, his face pinched, and he bit his tongue hard. Boiling water seemed to bubble in his throat, and he began to scream like he had last night. For a moment, an odd, worried look crossed Ellen's face But her other accomplice merely knelt beside him and placed her smallish hand upon his throat. Suddenly, Alexander felt as if a block of ice had been placed there. Clear as a bell, his voice rang out into the playground.

"Liar!" it cried to the heavens, "you tricked me you little…" The girl, whose proper name was Crystal, removed her hand at once and his speech became mindless screaming once again.

"You see?" crowed Alvin triumphantly, "we can free you from your pain, grant you power, or let you die."

Still shaking with pain and wonder, he was released completely.

"Go to the shadows at the playground's end and suffer no more" Alvin finished melodramatically, "any other path destroys you!"

He was filled with wonder. For a year, doctors at one of the city's best hospitals had tried to restore his voice and failed. How on earth had she done it? Abandoned in a corner of the field, he walked toward April, engrossed in memories.

A year ago, on this very field, Alexander had sat amidst the playground equipment thinking his life might finally change. That morning, when April and two other bullies began savagely pummeling him, Ellen leapt in the fray like a wildcat, pounding his abusers until they bled.

That had been the ninth time she had spared him the wrath of Sunrise's population of bullies, and his suspicions of her were fading quickly. When she wasn't fighting off his attackers Ellen was soft-spoken and shy. She had clasped his hand gently as they strolled toward the swing set and with each gentle push she slowly won his heart. By mid-recess, he was playing with her hair. Betrayal was far from his mind when she nervously asked

"C…could you do me a little favor, Alexander?" When he nodded energetically, she continued.

"I…I want to do something, and I'm certain it's not allowed but…" Alexander remembered turning to face her, curiosity and worry on his face. "It's nothing bad" Ellen replied hurriedly, "at least... I don't think so..."

After several questioning looks, she had whispered something in his ear. Immediately, his face broke into a hot blush at which Ellen couldn't help giggling. She pointed to a patch of shade near the enormous tree Alexander would have been hidden in that very minute without her and smiled softly.

"After school. Will you come?" As he neared that selfsame darkness, he saw his head bobbing vigorously.

April caught his right arm the minute he came within reach. A breeze began to whisper softly through the leaves scattering several strands of light brown hair across her face. She had been beside herself ever since Alvin had returned to announce Alexander's imminent arrival. Her eyes positively shone with greed and ambition as she tightened her grip.

"Hello, Mouse" she began eagerly, "I know why you're here. You want to know about your dreams, right?" Her voice was playful. She would enjoy this. "God only knows what terrors Lilith's whipped up for you; I certainly hope I never do." Alexander had begun to struggle with her hand, trying to get it near his throat. He desperately wanted to scream at her, to scare her into sharing her knowledge. But April's grip was firm.

"Aww, does baby wanna talk too?" she remarked teasingly, "because you can....if you do as you're told." Alexander had no intention of doing as he was told, a fact which the hatred etched upon his face conveyed perfectly. With his free arm, he caught a shock of his tormentor's hair, and as he yanked it savagely, he mouthed the words "tell me about the spirals. Now!"

Pain clouded April's face as she dug her nails into the flesh of his arm. She wasn't teasing any longer. She balanced herself and delivered a swift kick to Alexander's knee. When he faltered backwards she tore her hair from his clutches and began to speak in a low growl.

"I know why you have nightmares Alexander!" she roared, using his name for the first time in ages, "I know why you wake up screaming every morning." Alexander dove at her but she caught his foot with hers, and he fell to the ground. "I know why you can't talk" she continued, dodging Alexander's attempt at a sweeping kick, "what really happened to your friend"- she dodged a punch as he regained his feet, "Ms. Washington's car" –she eluded his grasp, "and your glasses" she finished, producing them with a flourish.

Alexander stopped struggling and stared at the apparition before him. He hadn't thought about his glasses for a long time but now that he saw them again a sudden empty longing consumed him. A desire to shield himself behind the heavy panes of glass began to seep into his consciousness and April observed confusion and wonder in his eyes.

Just a little more! she thought to herself. Today would not be like the last time. Alexander would yield today and she would gain the power to defy Helen.

Out loud, she asked "bet you'd like to know how I did that huh? After you saw me break them to bits." She smiled as Alexander nodded reluctantly. He still looked fierce, she noted, but he was weakening. She placed the glasses on his face, almost kindly, and he seemed tranquilized. Though curiosity lit his eyes, the anger was fading.

"You're beginning to understand, aren't you?" she asked quietly. "I have power. So do all of my, how did she put it… "little friends", that's right, all of us have power you could never imagine. We have the power to avoid trouble, or cause it and…to punish" she cried, more joyfully than she meant to.

"Ellen offered you that power when she brought you here." At the mention of Ellen's name Alexander's eyes darkened. "Struck a nerve, huh?" April laughed. "Well she had to do it. And so will you. A year ago, you stood here thoroughly confused. You wondered why your "friend" had brought you, and you weren't paying much attention. A girl named Susan Hollows told you about the Spiral Class. How Lilith started it when she came here, and how we have sworn to make this place better. She told you about Lilith's mysterious powers, how she

used them to fight bullying and bring peace to Sunrise."
Alexander gave April a dirty look here.

"We offered to change you. Ellen pleaded with you. But you were too stubborn" April hissed, anger creeping into her voice. "You wouldn't join a group of "stupid bullies". So you were punished." April smiled coldly as the memory invaded Alexander's mind. "It was fun to watch Ellen kiss you with her fist" she laughed. "Do you remember that?' Alexander gritted his teeth menacingly. He wanted to leap at April's throat, but she seemed close to revealing what he had come to learn, so he reined in his anger. April noticed this approvingly.

"Your dreams, the silence, Judith's "accident"… they're all punishments for not joining us. Do what you're told and I will consider setting you free from them. Otherwise, prepare to spend the rest of your life in terror."

Alexander felt the glasses that sat solidly on his face. They had been air a minute ago. He had spoken today for the first time in a year, a trick doctors throughout Miriam had failed to perform. The fears of the terrors he would face that night and the guilt he had felt by the stairwell were fresh in his mind, and at last, he turned to his mortal enemy, hatred blazing in his eyes. With great effort, he mouthed the words. "What do you want?" A cacophony of bells pealed across the playground declaring the end of recess, and April's victory.

It had been an extremely close call. Mr. Robert's description of his son's story, that April had carried Judith from the bench in full view of Ms. Prescott and beaten her under the astonished eyes of several spectators, had galvanized the outraged parents behind Aries' efforts to fire Emma, expel April, prosecute them both and investigate the school. Most of the children had omitted Emma from the tales they told their parents. They formed an uncomfortable semicircle around him and he began sweating as he stumbled ineffectively through his earlier assurances.

"No one came forward with such accusations yesterday!" he shouted defensively, as one insistent parent caught his shirt.

"And I can tell you why!" rang a confident, businesslike voice.

Amanda Phillips was a smart cookie. Her clear, concise judgments and powerfully analytical mind were respected, and sometimes feared, by her colleagues. Everything about her, from her tightly cropped, raven-tinted hair to the sharp, royal blue business suit she wore, echoed professionalism. When she stood to the right of Bellerose, he looked ancient and out of place. In unison, the collection of parents turned their gaze on her.

"I have learned" she began briskly, "that the children were coerced into making these charges". Several almost comical gasps of shock could be heard from the gathering. Ms. Washington's quiet celebrations were stilled by the mewing of a small child at the Principal's side. "Lucy here and others report being held in homeroom after recess instead of being sent on to Social Studies as usual. They assert that for the rest of the school day they were entreated by this instructor" she indicated Ms. Washington, "to revise the testimony they had provided to my vice-principal following the incident." Aries looked incredulous. "When this brave little girl brought this to my attention, I discovered her wrist was sprained. Badly. Which is a clear sign of…"

But they never learned what it was a clear sign of because the suddenly violent, yet eerily calm drawl of Daisy Fieldswallow, a pale wisp of womanhood without a trace of her daughter's timidness, interjected.

"If I find" she intoned, glaring at Aries, "that what she says is true, tell you what I'm gonna do. I'm gonna take you to your mama."

Mr. Roberts instantly fixed Mrs. Fieldswallow with a hateful glare and Aries, despite her outrage at the charges against her, was rapidly approaching a hue comparable to that of correction fluid.

Just over three decades ago, Aries' mother had been killed by the blast of an improvised explosive, which had shattered the glass of one of the house's rear windows. Most of Miriam had been fairly sure who was responsible but the police had been unwilling to prosecute Daisy's father and brother, fellow officers, and so the case was allowed to die.

"I hope" Ms. Phillips interjected firmly, "that nothing of the sort becomes necessary." A few parents nodded their agreement.

"I intimidated no one" Aries mumbled suddenly. "We didn't discuss the matter at all did we, Lucy dear?" The timid child shivered unhelpfully at the mention of her name. Aries tried again.

"I s…sent my class to Social Studies as Ms. Taylor will confirm." Lucy shook her tear stained little head, and Amanda replied like a mother who's just caught her daughter in a lie.

"According to Taylor, your entire class was absent." Aries' face registered genuine shock.

"B..but I…I sent" Amanda waved her hand for silence. Several parents were giving her evil looks.

"In addition" Amanda blazed on in triumph, "this note was written under duress!" She held up the letter Judith had given Alexander as Aries fumed at the injustice of it all.

"Despite several serious injuries and her viciously mangled hair, the author of this note and the victim of yesterday's attack remains in attendance. That fact, coupled with several extremely evident tear stains, allows me to reach the conclusion that…"

"I did nothing to my niece!" Aries shouted brutally. Lucy hiccupped. Ms. Fieldswallow's eyes bored into Aries with increasing hatred until the instructor replied plaintively, "I begged her to stay at home but she wouldn't hear of it. She was absolutely dead-set on showing everyone what April did to her."

"From detention?" Bellerose coughed loudly. "As I told you, she never left Ms. Chandler's sight." "Clearly, her niece came to school so Aries could keep our children lying via guilt."

Aries turned at once to face her accuser and was about to tell her off when she was silenced by Ms. Phillips.

"I have a child in the hall Ms. Washington that claims you took him on a little field trip yesterday. Against his will." Aries' heart sank as Alexander entered the room still looking everywhere but at her.

"I took care of you since kindergarten" she thought desperately, "I played with you, kept you from harm, found you a friend and made you perfect. Why are you doing this?"

Ms. Phillips stood Alexander next to Lucy.

"I can't wait to hear this one!" Mr. Roberts intoned. Ms. Phillips didn't' keep him waiting. She had been building up to this and she felt it was time to play the high card. She leapt into an explanation of Alexander's testimony and, moments later, Aries burst out of the teacher's lounge in tears.

"Sad, ain't it?"

The hoary old man leaned tiredly against the bulletproof glass that protected the cashiers at Johnny's Sub Shop. The sun shone in through wide windows, uncomfortably warming his liver-spotted skin as he casually skimmed through the Miriam Daily Voice. Beside him, a rotund woman with wild, faded hair considered the heavily amended menu taped to the glass.

"Sure is" she replied absently as two energetic little girls tugged at her skirts. "Funny what enough misery'll make a soul do. If it were any of my daughters..." She sighed heavily and let the sentence hang lazily in the air.

"I hear ya" the man replied, and he scratched his beard thoughtfully.

In just over a week, the meeting at Sunrise had become a budding scandal. Aries' mystic features were plastered upon the covers of Miriam's major newspapers and the town gossips speculated on each new headline with cruel impunity. Whether at home or the school, she was never safe from the city's armies of eager, young reporters, and the local police, led by the graying Detective Allen, patrolled the halls, took statements, and made notes for later review. It seemed to Aries that, ever since her departure from the teacher's lounge, her every thought, word and deed had been hurriedly scrawled in a notepad and published. Whenever she went anywhere stares of mingled pity and anger greeted her until she skulked into a corner in hope of some small refuge. Worst of all, both her mailbox and answering machine were spangled with threats she was certain came from Ms. Fieldswallow.

Others had become acquainted with Miriam's free press as well. For several days, the occupants of apartment 209 had become media darlings. Alexander was asked again and again to describe his harrowing trip to the hospital, the tests his teacher forced him to undergo, and the lies she made him tell to get them approved. The Miriam Daily Voice named him "a young man of singular courage."

The story only garnered more interest when, miraculously, Alexander's voice returned to him. Hannah was thrilled. She told the Daily Impartial that she'd "been considering legal action but since he started talking again I can't think of anything else."

By now, however, not even the joy of hearing her son for the first time in a year could make her tolerate one more set of questions.

"It's a lovely Saturday afternoon" she thought firmly, "and Alexander and I are going to enjoy it." Out loud, she gushed jubilantly. "I simply cannot believe it!" she cried, giving herself a theatrical pinch. "It's...it's just been so long." she sighed, hugging Alexander for the tenth time. "I'm so happy I could cry." Alexander chose not to mention that she was doing just that, and instead, tried desperately to mask the acid mix of guilt and sadness that was searing his heart. His voice had been returned to him for a steep price: the betrayal of his beloved teacher. He tried to convince himself that this was her just punishment for using his feelings for her to manipulate his behavior. But as Hannah continued her cheerful celebrations, Alexander began to feel as if he were sinking into a deep tar pit. Still, he struggled to smile as a sort of penance. His guardian, after all, hadn't celebrated anything in some time.

A gentle knocking jolted the young boy and caused his Rowan to swear rudely.

"Sorry, Alexander!" she exclaimed, clapping her hand over her mouth, and she marched toward the door with long, furious strides, her charge in tow.

The knocking stopped suddenly and Hannah earnestly hoped whoever was at the door had decided that no one was home. But the silence gave way to a melodic chime. Their visitor had merely discovered the doorbell. Sighing gravely, Alexander took the initiative. In a clear, ringing, voice he made a firm declaration.

"I am not, repeat NOT, giving any more interviews. Understand?"

"That's telling'em" Hannah thought proudly, but the muffled voice that replied shocked them both.

"I'm not a reporter" it rang sweetly, "I'm a little girl."

Hannah was curious. Miriam's local Girl Scout troop wasn't due for some time and no one had ever come to visit Alexander in all the time she could remember. Eager to solve this mystery, she opened the door, and indeed, bathed in insufficient light, a little girl stood before them.

"It's a miracle!" Hannah laughed to herself.

The "miracle" in question was slightly taller than Alexander. Her face, normally peach-toned, looked dingy in the half-light of the hallway. This was made up for by two brilliant blue eyes that seemed to radiate innocence. She was dressed in a serviceable pair of black and white high-tops, a stylish pair of black jeans with plenty of pockets, an overlarge white tee shirt depicting "The Swift Detectives", and a chromatic friendship bracelet. But Hannah was drawn to her willful strawberry blond hair, which shot off in all sorts of inviting angles like a wild growth. She took an instant liking to the wonder in her hallway and, with politeness exceptional in an often-frazzled nurse, ushered her inside.

"Now how can I help you?" Hannah asked kindly. In the more robust light of the apartment, evidence of tears became visible on each of her pouty cheeks. "And why have you been crying?" Hannah found sadness hard to imagine on such a momentous day.

In answer, the child's eyes began welling with fresh tears and Hannah knelt quickly to catch her in a comforting hug. It was then she noticed Alexander was gone.

"Now where did he get to?" she asked the room. The child wiped her eyes with her arm, gulped, and answered morosely.

"He left when he saw me, and I don't blame him." Hannah gave her a bemused look.

"Don't be silly. Alexander wouldn't do anything that rude." She began to call for him, but the little girl caught Hannah's hand and shook her head.

"He won't come." she said with certainty. "He'd rather be punished. Ms. Phillips threatened to expel him once, and he still wouldn't come near me."

"And why not?" Hannah cried, outraged. "Why I have a mind to..." But Ellen shook her head again.

"Believe me" she whimpered, "I deserve it. My name is Ellen Lockett" she rushed, before Hannah could interrupt, "I did something terrible to Alexander. Really, really, really, really, really, really bad, and I cane to say I'm sorry." As she broke into a fresh bout of crying, Hannah rocked her gently.

"Come now", she consoled, "it can't be as bad as you make it sound."

Wriggling free, Ellen fished a crumpled dollar from one of her many pockets.

"Wanna bet?" she asked, smiling weakly.

Eager to hear the tale and tell her she was overreacting, Hannah nodded. Ellen sighed deeply.

"I made him think I liked him" she began with emphasis. "Then, I promised to kiss him after...that's not the bad part" she said quickly, when Hannah glared at her involuntarily, "The bad part is when he came..." Ellen shook her head.

"Well?" asked Hannah after a long pause.

"I...I took him to the end of the playground where the bullies were waiting...." Her voice trailed.

"And they beat him up" Hannah finished slowly. Ellen shook her head no.

"They held him down..." she wept bitterly.

"Then who...you mean…oh dear!"

Hannah stared at the little girl and handed her a dollar.

"I told you so" she sighed frowning. Hannah shook her head.

"Can you tell me why you pummeled my child?" she asked, trying to maintain her former tone. Ellen nodded.

"There's a girl at our school named April. She's mean. Really really…"

"I get the picture" Hannah interrupted quickly. Ellen nodded.

"She's got a cool club, and if you join, no one can hurt you and you always have a bunch of friends. I wanted in more than anything. April promised I could get in if I...I'm really sorry."

For some reason, Hannah believed her.

"Alright" she said softly, "calm down now. How are you going to apologize if Alexander won't listen?"

"I don't know" Ellen quietly admitted, "but I have to try."

Hannah wondered at the odd look in her guest's eyes, but nodded and called Alexander. When he didn't respond, she called twice more. After two more tries, she excused herself and, presently, a lively din could be heard. Moments later, Ellen strived with every fiber in her being to suppress the laughter bubbling within her as Hannah returned carrying her son like an overgrown baby.

When Alexander gave up struggling, she put him down gently and the second he was free, he turned away from Ellen.

"Rowan may be buying her goody-two-shoes act" Alexander thought bitterly, "but Ellen isn't fooling me twice!"

Grasping his shoulders, Hannah physically turned him to face his teary eyed foe. She began to let him go but Alexander made to dash for the hallway and she realized she'd have to hold him in place for the entire conversation.

"You don't think you're overreacting at all?" she sighed.

Predictably, Alexander shook his head. He was certain Ellen had left her role in his yearlong silence out of whatever story she told Rowan.

"She ruined second grade" he mumbled. "She never stopped making fun of me."

Ellen had forgotten about that. April had carried the story of Alexander's misadventure throughout Sunrise, forcing him to put up with vicious taunting, and the occasional kick in the shins, at every turn. When she thought of all the terrible things she had been made to say to him since then, she glanced longingly at the door and wished she hadn't come.

"Well, she came to apologize for that, Alexander" Hannah replied, "and I'd appreciate it if I didn't have to hold you here for it. Now I'm going to the kitchen, and I expect you to stay put." And with that, Hannah released him. Remarkably, he didn't move. Satisfied, she strode across the living room and in short order, disappeared from sight.

Tuckered out from the long walk and all the crying she'd done, Ellen quietly sat on the end of Hannah's wide, beige sofa that was closest to her. Mumbling vehemently, Alexander gave her a wide berth and took a seat on the opposite end, as far from her as was possible. Ellen frowned.

"I had to do it" she sighed. "You know how April is. Once I agreed to trick you she didn't let me change my mind."

The kitchen was well within earshot and Alexander wanted this nuisance gone as quickly as possible. So he leaned toward her slightly and whispered "Liar! You could have done whatever you wanted. April said the same thing, and I didn't believe her either. "

"I didn't want..." Ellen replied meekly, but Alexander cut her off.

"Yes you did" he asserted harshly, forgetting to whisper.

There was a loud stirring in the kitchen, and Alexander sat up nervously.

"Lilith is heartless when she's upset" Ellen whispered urgently. "I..I had to…"

Alexander paid no attention to the fear that had crept into Ellen's voice.

"Who's Lilith and what does she have to do with you?" he queried much more quietly. He remembered what April had said about a person by that name causing all his misery.

Ellen opened her mouth to answer but stopped when Hannah approached with milk and cookies. She gave Alexander a fierce stare as she placed these delicacies on the coffee table, and vanished down the hall.

Ellen nervously reached for a cookie. "Lilith is a girl." she said, taking a bite. "Well... at least she used to be. When she came to Sunrise she was like everyone else. She got beaten up and picked on every day and she had no friends at all. But one day, she was getting kicked in the stomach by some girl and sort of snapped. She stood up and pointed at the girl, and the poor thing started to dry out and crack. Everyone was screaming for the grown ups but no one came, and that little girl almost died. After that, people left Lilith alone."

Ellen sighed deeply and grabbed a new cookie as if she needed the sugar to continue. "I couldn't change my mind. She would have hurt me. Badly."

Alexander glared at her, determined not to understand.

"So better me than you, huh?" he spat hatefully.

Slowly, Alexander began to feel happier. True, he had lied and accepted undeserved sympathy and praise, but there were still people worse than him.

"I didn't hurt anyone like she did" he told himself.

"Look, I had to do it!" Ellen replied defensively, "and I came here to apologize for all the trouble I caused. I thought you'd understand now". Indignation suddenly flared into her eyes. "How is what you did to Ms. Washington worse than what I did to..."

"I didn't lie to her" he replied quickly. "I didn't make her think we were friends!" As he said this, his anger at Ms. Washington came rushing back. So far, two people had used his emotions to control him and, seething in his seat, he decided he wasn't taking it anymore.

But Ellen had had enough.

"You be sure to tell Judith that when she's in foster care!" she shot back angrily.

She was sick of apologizing and explaining herself. Her crimes were legion, but she had to make him understand why she had come. As she watched him, the redness in his cheeks seemed to fade as his face relaxed visibly. Alexander had no answer for her and she knew it. He hadn't thought of just how big a lie he'd told. Alexander suddenly realized that he had destroyed two lives, and a deep depression settled over him. It was his turn to cry.

When Ellen saw the first tears fall, a sudden current rushed through her heart. Tentatively, she inched herself closer, almost smiling when Alexander kept his seat.

"I lied to you and I'm sorry" she said one last time. "I didn't know you then and I was only interested in impressing April. The others made it sound like a dream" she sighed, remembering, "I could have anything I wanted, I'd never be bullied again...friends" she shook her head. "They promised me friends."

"And did you make any?" Alexander asked gloomily.

"Yes" she replied, inching closer, "you were a great friend. I missed you"

Alexander looked up, thoroughly surprised. Even since she had "pleaded" with him to join the Spiral Class, she had always given him the impression that she hated him.

"I tried to convince April to let me out of it" she continued, "even offered her the powers back. She just told me to shut up and do what I was told."

Alexander looked directly at her for the first time

"You have powers?" he asked suddenly excited. Ellen nodded solemnly.

"Just how do you think I rescued you from all those bullies?"

Alexander was barely listening.

"Can you get rid of the nightmares?" he asked hurriedly. "If you can, I'll forgive you, we'll be friends, whatever you wa...huh?" Alexander's eyes widened in shock.

Ellen had finally managed to inch herself beside him and, wearing an expression of silent joy, she hugged him tightly. Red as a beet, he struggled within her grasp.

"Wh...What are you doing?" he cried, almost scared.

"Hugging you." she answered softly. "I can't cure your nightmares but I still want to be your friend."

In a dismal corner of a tiny bedroom, Aries slumped miserably in a faded armchair and fervently prayed the reporters outside couldn't see her. She had drawn thick, white curtains over every window in the house, but she worried the brilliant light of the Saturday morning sun was betraying her shadow. All morning, her phone had rung savagely. She'd answered the first few times, and was immediately startled by gruff voices barking loaded questions. Soon she had forbidden Judith to answer the phone, and it now lay in pieces near the living room wall she had hurled it against.

But demolishing it hadn't stopped the constant pounding. People representing the Voice, the Impartial, and a dozen other city newspapers battered her door relentlessly. At first, Aries had tried pretending she was not at home, but her visitors remained persistent. The steady noise was oppressing Judith who clutched madly at her head and shook as her eyes watered painfully. In the end, a neighbor had called the police to chase them from her front steps. Now they had returned to set a sort of ambush and Aries hid behind her curtains cursing Alexander.

Based on his lies, Ms. Phillips had unceremoniously cast her from the teacher's lounge, and her job, pending further investigation. Despite Judith's condition, she had been declined pay during the suspension period. She groaned heavily, gleaning her mind for an answer to Judith's worsening injuries. Her last visit to Sunrise had claimed the last of her savings.

"How could anyone be so heartless?" she wondered as a low moan wafted across the hall. "How could the students, my students, tell such nightmarish lies?" And then she was struck by a violent memory.

"Your little friends don't scare me."

Was this April's promised revenge? Aries racked her brains and struggled to remember whether Lucy had been a part of the gaggle of students she had challenged so often. The answer eluded her. It didn't matter No one would believe her.

"How did she convince Alexander?" she wondered. "He couldn't possibly have been that angry." She shook her head like a sorrowful Saint Bernard and buried it in her hands, crying softly.

Across the hall, Judith was far too occupied with keeping her aunt from discovering how much pain she was suffering to care about anything else. Each night shattering glass, relentless bullets, and her mother's blood-choked screams of pain rocked her dreams. She had ripped several holes in her blankets and that morning her curtain rod became as bare as Alexander's. But unlike him, her broken legs confined her to a lonely twin bed that made staying awake only slightly better. Though she did not constantly have to relive her parents' death, her legs grew sore and swollen. She was beginning to worry about the blood that still trickled from her nose. She had no idea how much she needed to live but she was sure her nosebleed wasn't healthy. Every now and then, she felt wildly dizzy but she avoided lying down for fear of falling asleep. Heavy purplish bags had grown under her eyes, which had swollen almost shut and stung so horribly that, at that moment, she was screaming into a pillow so Aries wouldn't hear. And the constant knocking was making her head feel as if someone were sitting on it. Suddenly, it was replaced by an impressive string of expletives as her aunt tore open he front door.

But the person she was swearing at was not an eager reporter. A tall, businesslike black woman stood in her doorway sporting meticulously braided hair, a crisp black suit, a thin pair of spectacles, and a bitter frown. Aries leapt back in shock and sputtered to explain herself but the woman waved her into silence.

"Quiet, Washington!" she ordered harshly. "Time is precious. " She stepped briskly past Aries, who shut the door. "Care to explain that mess?" the newcomer barked, indicating the pile of rubbish that was once the phone. "Never mind" she cut in as Aries prepared to reply. You know why I'm here. Currently, you lack the finances and access to medical care Judith desperately needs, your home is no longer a stable environment conducive to the psychological health of the child, and you may well be an unstable individual who poses a danger to herself and others. Frankly" she laughed sharply, "I am not sure why I haven't been ordered to remove Judith from your care." Aries breathed a relieved sigh. "Soft-hearted managers most likely" she opined. "In any case, as you may know, you have been convicted in the court of public opinion and therefore, my bosses can only ignore Judith's needs until the trial is completed. At that point, if these conditions remain, or if you are found guilty, Judith will come with me. Understand?" she finished coldly.

Hannah's voice was choked with a mix of fear and rage, so she nodded silently.

"Good." Ms. Washington replied coldly, "Let's visit Judith."

Monday morning arrived to blood curdling screams. Hannah had yet to affix new curtains so a bright patch of sun illuminated her madly flailing child. She had hoped his renewed voice was a herald of the end of his nightmares but no such good fortune had befallen them. Yet, as she rocked Alexander into silence, a smile played across her full lips.

"I've got a surprise for you" she giggled to herself. And breakfast that morning was a happier affair.

"So" she began playfully, "did that little girl kiss you the other day?" Pretending to focus on cutting her eggs, she struggled to hide her laughter as some of Alexander's breakfast sprayed from his crimson face.

"Absolutely not!" he sputtered as soon as he was able. "That's disgusting. She's a girl" He sounded as if he was discussing the logic of having a pet skunk. Desperately, he hoped Hannah hadn't seen Ellen hugging him.

"Well what's wrong with girls?" she asked in a voice of mock offense. Alexander chewed rapidly and swallowed hard. Then with a deathly serious expression on his round, inviting face, he asserted with certainty "girls are evil."

Hannah nearly choked on her pancake.

"Well they are" he replied defensively as Hannah's coughs gave way to voluminous laughter. Alexander was glad to see joy in his guardian's face but he wasn't kidding. He thought of all the suffering two girls in particular had wrought.

"And whhh...."Hannah fought for breath. "what if you had to walk to school with one?" Alexander stopped eating to stare into Rowan's watery eyes, a look of stunned fear woven in his face. "You didn't...." he stammered weakly. "Please tell me you didn't", he begged. The doorbell rang and Alexander nearly fainted.

Hannah half expected him to dart angrily toward his room, but Alexander did a curious thing. Shaking badly, he marched toward the door. Slowly, trance-like, he removed the chain, turned the lock, and pulled back the door to reveal Ellen Lockett smiling nervously in the hall.

With a quick peck to Alexander's forehead, Hannah shot down the hall in a fit of giggles. The two stared at each other for several moments, and then, Ellen broke her silence.

"Do you still hate me?"

He considered this, and shook his head slowly.

"I...missed you" he replied hypnotically. "Sort of." And in a quiet surrender to fate, they held hands and marched soberly down the hall.

Happily, they were empty for once and Alexander allowed himself to be led by Ellen as his mind wandered back to the swings. Timidly, his fingers had woven in and out of her silken, flower-scented hair as she rocked back and forth slowly, a complacent smile on her face. The world had seemed right then. Despite the endless bullies, the horrible nightmares, the lack of a voice...he had been happy. As she led him into the stairwell, he began to wonder if she could do it again. Could she make him forget his betrayals? Teach him a way around Lilith's mysterious powers. Could she make his life bearable once more? Alexander heard the door slam behind them, though in his mind he was wrapping his fingers in strawberry tresses. A moment later, Ellen's mouth fell open in surprise as a thick, wizened hand clasped Alexander's throat. "

Well iffit ana lil' screamin boy" a raggedy voice croaked joyfully. Alexander tried to avoid the hot clouds of liquor tainted breath that followed every word. "Done finly mestup huh now? I gotcha an I'ma beat all that screamin outcha today!"

"You let him go!" Ellen shouted firmly as Dottie's free hand came into view. She had apparently recovered from whatever had ailed her because it held a thick, folded leather belt like a vise. Struggling against his captor, Alexander turned his head to face Ellen.

"RUN!!" he yelled savagely, but Ellen closed her eyes instead.

"Betta do what he say lil' gal." Dottie remarked evilly. "Lessen acourse you wan some too."

Alexander thrashed violently as Dottie raised her weapon, savoring the moment. Bare hatred flared in her eyes. She intended to pay him back for a year of sleepless nights. Then, all at once, Alexander seemed to ripple in and out of focus.

"Wha....?" Alexander asked, terrified. "Ellen what's happ..." And in that pause, his features melted into light and he was gone. Dottie gave such a nightmarish scream then that Ellen tore down the steps without another word.

At the bottom she leapt through the back door and searched with her eyes for a concealed space. Spotting the overhanging branches that led to Arcadia Park, Ellen dived into the shadows and shut her eyes once more.

"Come back to me" she whispered, and the air quivered around her. She smiled as six streams of golden light began to flow into a ball at their center. The sphere, which was the size of a marble, grew rapidly. Its surface was soon covered with cracks through which shafts of light escaped to freedom.

"Come on" Ellen whispered eagerly, and at last, the ball burst into millions of light particles revealing Alexander who stared at her in wonder.

"W..where was I?" he asked weakly. "You...sa...how?" Ellen knelt beside him, patting his head gently.

"I told you I had powers" she smiled. "That was Elysium, sort of a pocket in reality. It's a really good hiding place. " She began to walk toward the entrance but Alexander didn't move.

"Come on" she cried. "We'll be..." She had turned to help him up but the look in his eyes halted her. It was a look not of simple gratitude, but of indescribable joy. At last, he stood, wobbled, and straightened himself. And he took her hand in his.

"Thanks" he breathed dizzily, and he turned into the shade.

"We can't go that way" Ellen said at once. "I used to live here. We'll fall and kill ourselves." Alexander shook his head.

"We'll be careful. Just keep your balance and..."

"But its so much safer the normal way" Ellen interrupted. "I don't think anyone will bother you if that's what you're worried about." But Alexander shook his head and all joy fled his face. In that moment, truth seized Ellen's heart.

"What do you see over there?" she asked slowly. "What does she show you? It's only an illusion." she consoled, "It won't..."

"There's a girl" Alexander cut in fearfully, "in a blue dress and she's..." With an intake of breath, Ellen clapped her hand over his mouth and they turned down the path.

"How did April get her powers?" Alexander asked, gingerly kicking a bramble out of Ellen's way.

"Well, she was tough" she sighed deeply. "When she showed up in first grade, she never talked to anyone. She sat in corners and stared at the walls until the teacher gave her something to do. People teased her a lot and pummeled her at recess but she never, ever cried. She just curled into a little ball"

"That's kind of creepy" Alexander commented. Ellen nodded and ducked under a branch.

"Well, Lilith was impressed by it. She had a little talk with April near the big tree on the playground. After that, no one ever bothered her again. Odd things began to happen. Somebody's lesson plan would vanish, a bunch of students would mutiny...a teacher was threatened for the first time ever. His name was Mr. Bellows. He sent a bunch of Lilith's friends to detention for threatening other students." Ellen lowered her voice. "April took revenge. She set the school on fire."

Alexander looked at her, surprised.

"But Bill did that. Didn't he?" She shook her head.

"Everyone remembered his fireballs in kindergarten. They sent him to counseling, and April went free."

The faint, brown river of mud and stone came into view and Alexander cried out a warning. Ellen watched him steady himself against the wall of trees that was rapidly forming. She walked behind him, copying his actions.

"Lilith reined her in" Ellen continued slowly, "but she became really popular with troublemakers so Lilith used April to organize them. Now they basically run half the school."

"And no one tries to stop them?" Alexander asked incredulously. "Not even you?" Ellen just shook her head.

"The fire spooked the teachers and the new principal something awful, and I'm just not brave enough." She shivered badly, thinking of Alexander's vision. "You're just about the only person who isn't terrified of April's power. I think that's why she wants you."

"Well, she can't have me!" Alexander replied firmly, shuffling along the narrowest part of the path. "I won't hurt anyone else".

In reply, or so it seemed to Alexander, Ellen placed one of her hands on each of his shoulders. Instantly, more currents ran through him and he grew slightly dizzy "I don't want to fall," she said by way of explanation, but she didn't immediately let go when the path turned to the park.

Arcadia Park was nearly deserted and all its pleasures lay tantalizingly before them. Springy emerald grasses, rolling hills, swings, and huge slides... all of it begged to be played with. Unbeknownst to Alexander, Ellen had made up her mind about something she'd been informed of Hannah's call yesterday morning. She sat in the first bench she saw and started untying her off-white high tops.
"What in the world are you doing?" Alexander cried, running up to her. "We'll be late for class!"

"Uh-uh" she laughed mischievously, "because we're not going."

She kicked off her left shoe and started on her right. Alexander stared at her in disbelief.

"We have to go!" he exclaimed. "or we'll be punished." He watched her slip her right foot free. Next she attacked her socks.

"I'll get you out of whatever trouble you get in," she promised. "You'll have fun, and no one will know the difference. And besides" she laughed, playing her high card, "you forgot your book bag."

A look of horror crossing his face, Alexander felt around his chest where the straps should have been and found she was right. He made a dive for the narrow path but Ellen caught his arm. She hadn't expected this much resistance.

"Why do you want to go so much?" she asked. "You know you'll hate it. They'll question you all day, and people'll bully you."

He knew she was right, and his dizzied brain was running out of counterpoints. Then something occurred to him.

"You can use your powers to..."

"I won't do it" she interrupted quickly. Alexander sighed heavily. First he had lied about Ms. Washington, and now he was skipping class. But he realized he had no choice in the matter and removed his shoes as she ran through the grass around him. Neither of them saw the tiny figure that watched from the tallest slide.

Helen Greywiche sat at the vice-Principal's desk worriedly thumbing through student files. For the second time, she was desperately trying to rein in the damage from April's abuse of power. Rather than take responsibility for Judith's injuries, as she had been ordered to, April had told a lie which was spiraling out of control. Despite her dire warnings following the fire, Miriam's finest patrolled the halls. Worse, newspaper and even local television reporters were woven throughout Sunrise. She had precious little time to use whatever she could find to scare the school into silence. Because if her true intentions were ever discovered, she would never be forgiven. As this thought entered her mind, she snapped to attention and tore through the files so intently that she did not hear the soft footfalls that drew nearer each second.

"Are we busy, Ms. Greywiche?" Helen froze at the deeply arrogant voice. It implied high society and old money, though its owner could currently claim neither.

"It cannot be," she thought desperately. "He can't be here". But as she turned toward the voice, fear caught in her throat, and she thought she now understood the feelings she inspired in others.

"S...S...Samuel!" she struggled, choking on the word. "Y...you aren't supposed to be here. The D...d...d...director sai..."

"I care not what she says, and you know it" Samuel cut in harshly. "What matters" he intoned, absently brushing a shock of black hair from his right eye, "is that amateurs are failing miserably to do the work of experts, wasting time and resources, and risking secrecy." Helen made to speak, but was silenced by a dark glance from Samuel. "You have, so far, had two years to deliver to the Institute, two small children, aged eight years old. You have failed. In addition, the mission is now on the verge of discovery.

"No one will know" Helen interrupted, panicking. "I have the school under my..."

"The school was never your mission!" Samuel growled menacingly. "But undeserved power has made you forget this. Still" he spoke more calmly, "that power is not your own and I shall claim it in due course."

Helen shook badly at this. He pointed upward suddenly, and she shot out of her chair as if a geyser had been beneath her.

"In the meantime, you will deliver the Elements to me. If you are refused once more, I shall rend you asunder! Do we understand each other?" he asked coldly. Helen nodded.

"He'll join us..." she squeaked, terrified, "he has nowhere else to go!" With a savage smile, Samuel broke her nose.

Molly raced towards her classroom at breakneck speed, her chest heaving with the effort. Once inside, she paused briefly to watch Bill and Emily cautiously approach their lockers. Their eyes filled with dread when the pair felt her gaze.

Ever since the afternoon Molly had arrived to find her cubby empty, she'd introduced fire ants into Bill and Emily's book bags, lunchboxes and pencil cases. Ms. Washington had failed to discover the culprit before her suspension, and her replacement didn't seem to care, so instead of going to his cubby, Bill faced his least favorite student and mumbled, barely audibly.

"I'm sorry I took your things. You'll get'em all back. I'll never do it again." She nodded. Full of pride, however, Emily dove into her things without another word. Seconds later, she emerged swearing as loudly as she dared, and covered in ants. Molly wasted no more time, but dived toward the far end of the room, where Ms. Washington's replacement sat reading a romance novel.

"Ms. Hall" she remarked at her pupil's approach, "you are to retrieve our text, Notes on Penmanship, and begin reading." She couldn't see the dirty look Molly gave her through the rose-scented pages.

"Since you don't take attendance" Molly began, "you may not realize it, but you have a truant on your hands and it's your duty..."

"Never mind that, Molly. Take a seat" Ms. Prescott replied dismissively.

"At this moment" Molly continued as if she hadn't heard Emma, "Alexander is in the park dancing about with some girl and..."

"And I don't care" Emma interjected without looking up, "not even a little bit. Now sit down" she finished firmly.

"And how will Lilith react when she finds you've left the little liar on his own to suffer an attack of conscience and tell someone the truth?" Molly asked hotly.

Emma shut her novel at once.

"People can hear you!" she whispered fretfully. "Goodness knows who's listening. Fine, you little brat. Take a seat and I'll go get him." Molly smiled, satisfied, as Ms. Prescott trudged toward the door.

"How on Earth did I let you talk me into this?" Alexander was clinging for dear life to the metal rail of a crowded subway train. Outside, the lights blurred as the cars raced toward an unknown destination.

"Relax" Ellen cried happily. "We're perfectly fine. Besides, you'll thank me when we get there." Thankfully, no one had recognized him so far. Still, Alexander wasn't certain he'd be thanking her if Hannah ever found out about this. They had left all of Miriam behind them, and in mere moments, all of Maryland would follow. For his first subway ride ever, Ellen had already taken him further from home than he had ever gone.

The swiftly passing lights reminded him forcibly of his mother. When Alexander was three, his favorite thing in the world to do had been marveling at the lights as Alma Lightarrow drove through a tunnel. He could see himself giggling merrily as she hummed "We Gather Together", her favorite song. A nostalgic sort of sadness soon consumed Alexander. Since Hannah never talked about his mother, he hadn't thought of her in ages, but suddenly, he had a deep desire to see her again. Still, Alexander was old enough to know that kind of wish was never granted.

At last the train screeched to a halt on the outskirts of Virginia.

"This won't end well" Alexander mumbled as he followed Ellen up an enormous escalator.

"Of course it will!" she laughed brightly. He got the impression she had done this before. They emerged on one end of an eight-lane highway. On the other end was little kid heaven. Alexander hugged Ellen involuntarily.

A small army of schoolchildren might have dreamed up contessa's Candy Castle. It featured a massive arcade, a restaurant that specialized in burgers and pizza, and an unparallel ice cream shop. Alexander's eyes grew wide with longing and Ellen laughed as they dashed along the crosswalk.

"Would you still rather go to class?" she asked cheerfully. Alexander shook his head no.

On the threshold, Alexander noticed a sign that read,

"Children will not be admitted without parent(s)."

He turned to Ellen to point this out but she had shut her eyes already.

"Just remember to call me "mommy" every now and then." she said once she opened them. "Cause to everyone else, I'll look like one." He stared at her skeptically, finding that difficult to swallow, but they entered without incident.

A moment later, her mouth stuffed with cheese pizza, Ellen realized she was really happy for the first time in ages. She had finally found a good use for the powers she had bartered her soul for. Here, underneath a stain glass chandelier, she had finally found peace.

Chapter Three: The Shades of War

Hidden in the shade of the trees near Cradle, and another less natural veil, a flustered Ms. Prescott addressed young April Rainer.

"Playtime is over, young lady," she began. "The city is watching our every move, the school's being investigated and Lilith is in a bitter mood. On top of it, I have to pretend I can teach, listen to that Grigori girl whine, and baby-sit your liars. Now, you little troublemaker, where is Alexander?"

"You won't like the..."

"Just tell me where!" Emma interrupted. "What kind of spies are the Grigori if they can't find a little boy?"

"I wouldn't know" April replied coolly, "I'm not one of them. Their last reports had him at Contessa's in Virginia, but he has since vanished from sight."

"What do you mean "vanished"?" Emma asked hotly. "Lilith wants him converted today!"

"Well that may not be possible!" April snapped. "They say some sort of incident occurred there."

Children screamed for their mothers as posters and hangings caught fire. Thick, black smoke poured from the arcade room, which was being lapped up by electrical fires. A pale, dark-haired specter cut tables, chairs and lamps, and in a corner, rattling with fear, Alexander was wondering what had gone wrong. Mere moments earlier, he had finally accepted his situation, finally embraced the ideals of unbridled fun Ellen had tried to show them. Now, their wonderland was a living, burning hell from which neither could easily escape.

Beside him, pressed beneath the smoke, Ellen shut her eyes in a fourth attempt to draw them into the safety of Elysium. But the agonized screams of the injured and dying were affecting her concentration, and then, the menace stood before them. He wore skintight white armor that looked as if it were made of one unbroken sheet of metal. It seemed quickened with a life of its own and Alexander doubted that anything could make it yield. His skin was pale as the face of the moon. The very eyes seemed cloaked in death. It spoke with dreadful arrogance in a voice that carried over the desperate cries of newly childless mothers.

"I shall ask once!" he cried, producing a katana and placing the sharp edge at Ellen's throat. "Then you will die." Tears streaming down her face, Ellen began silently praying. But crawling from his corner, spangled with ash, Alexander got to his feet.

"Leave her alone!" he ordered loudly, not knowing where this sudden burst of bravado was coming from. "Let her go!" The invader smiled darkly.

"I am Samuel, little boy. I command the Spiral Society that has hunted your kind for decades. Your parents, and hundreds of others, died on my orders." Alexander tensed visibly here. "You will kneel and serve me or..."

"Or you'll kill Ellen. Right?" Alexander interrupted fiercely.

"Wrong" Samuel spat. "I'll torture her instead!"

At that, unable to think of another solution, Alexander fell to his knees.

"Wise choice, Alexander!" Samuel laughed. "But remember this: I do not know mercy." With that, he raised his weapon and prepared to strike. One parent dared to run to her rescue, but with a wave of his finger, Samuel impaled her on a bolt of lightning. Then the blade roared down in a swift arc and Alexander shut his eyes. Seconds later a jarring metallic sound made them bolt open.

White streams of light were issuing from his hands and weaving themselves into a tight bubble around Ellen whose eyes were wide with shock. Samuel tossed aside his badly dented sword and grabbed Alexander by the throat.

"I am always glad of proof." he muttered, and as the ceiling collapsed, he vanished.

All of this had taken only ten minutes, and when fire crews arrived, they were horrified at the damage. They hacked through the remnants of the building, dutifully noting each loss of life, and combating the remaining flames. The only joyful moment was when Stephen "Spyglass" Smith discovered a feebly coughing mass.

"Over here!" he called to his fellows, and they cleared debris with singular purpose. When they heard Ellen's story, it was attributed to delirium. Looking about, Smith hoped this "Alexander" was an imaginary friend.

The school office's clock struck 3:15 and students tore out of Sunrise with relish. The autumn leaves were just beginning to fall but no one paid them the slightest attention. Most of them were trampled underfoot by children eager to escape their prison. Inside, Emma Prescott thought she knew how they felt. She would have given anything to escape her situation. She stood before the vice Principal's desk, flanked by April and Molly. Facing them was an imposing shadow that they had all come to fear.

"So" it began coldly, "what you mean to say, Prescott is that in addition to the consequences of April's cowardice, we cannot complete our plans, and Hall here isn't even certain Alexander remains alive?"

Molly's stomach was tangled in knots as Emma nodded slowly. She prepared to sink into blackness and sorrow but instead of growing angry, Helen surprised everyone by seeming to go into deep thought. As she pondered, they stood warily about, trying to judge her mood. At last, she sat straight in her chair and laughed. It was an unnerving, hollow sound.

"We have played around enough." she remarked suddenly. "Your new orders will be followed exactly as given or I will punish you severely." April and Emma saw flashes of a small girl in a blue dress waft through their minds, but Molly looked restless.

"Rainer, you will find the press and tell them that you beat up Judith, broke Lucy's wrist, and forced people to lie to protect you. Should be easy enough. It's the truth. Prescott, you are to arrange the kidnapping of the new girl, Judith. She will replace Alexander in our plans. Hall, you will..."

"I don't work for you!" Molly yelled tearfully. "My "salary" is dead, remember?" April and Prescott turned to their compatriot, who began to blush as she realized what she had admitted. But Helen starred hatefully at the teary-eyed thing before her.

"Do as you are told, Molly, and you will not have to join him." Molly's skin started to ripple and she screamed uncontrollably. Pinholes began to pockmark her skin and small shafts of what looked like sunlight shot through effortlessly. Ten seconds later, Molly held up her hands in surrender. The pain stopped at once.

"You will visit what's left of Contessa's to determine what really happened."

Molly wanted to know how kidnapping Judith would further the ideas Helen claimed to uphold, but the pain she had suffered was fresh in her mind and the three allowed themselves to be dismissed.

Alexander was veiled in darkness. His neck throbbed and the ropes that bound him to a frigid, metal table were biting into his flesh. Several thoughts ran through his mind at once. Where was Ellen? Was she alright? What had Samuel meant by "your kind"? Was he lying about killing his parents? Hannah had never explained why he didn't have a proper mother and father. Was this why? And , strangest of all, how had he made the bubble that had protected Ellen. These thoughts were silenced by the voice of his captor.

"I suppose you may be wondering just how you spared your friend my blade" he began calmly, as if he had read Alexander's mind. "That is simple enough. Some time ago, an evolution was unnaturally forced upon humanity. The nature of this adaptation allows one to achieve, by manipulation of mental energy, what would otherwise be impossible. The possible applications for this energy are potentially limitless. Those who have developed this evolution are referred to as Elements. Your mother was an Element. Therefore, so are you. This is why she is dead and you are here. Alexander struggled with his bonds.

"Obviously, chaos would be the most significant result of allowing such an evolution to continue unchecked. Therefore, the Spiral Society exists to control those Elements who will bow to reason, and to destroy the remainder." Alexander tried to protest this logic, but his voice failed him. At first, he thought he had fallen into silence once more, but he soon realized he'd been gagged. Apparently, Samuel wished to be sure he was uninterrupted.

"You are here because there are those who feel this duty is no longer necessary, or rather, that it is not we who must perform it. Until quite recently, you were part of their plan to usurp our authority. Yet I have seen evidence of a change in plan. War is at my doorstep young one, and willing or not, you will serve at my side."

That moment, a flash of white light shattered the darkness as Alexander leapt from the table, suddenly free. He dived at Samuel as if launched from a cannon, full of rage at the things he had heard. But his anger could not equal Samuel's skill and with a snap of his fingers, a beam of light hit Alexander's throat like a brick and sent him gasping to the floor. "You may understand power, Alexander" he growled, "but I am not" Samuel murmured, "a little girl."

About an hour to the west of the library was an odd sight. Salem's Point was a community associated with dust. No other place in the city was so saturated with it. Whenever one looked at this particular locale, the first thought that came to mind was always "who would choose to live here?" Known for ragged streets, misshapen buildings, and general ugliness, Salem's Point was considered by many to be an eyesore on the general city. More that one mayor had suggested condemning the entire area. And yet, few residents complained. The Pointers, as they were called, seemed to view their dingy hamlet with pride. One exception to this could be found in a run down maroon townhouse at 1704 Shylock Place. For that address belonged to Sunrise's illustrious vice-principal, Allen Bellerose.

Bellerose shuffled through his cramped living room at what was, for him, remarkable speed. He was certain his efforts were pointless, but he wanted every barrier possible between him and the madman. He had locked and re-locked every door and window in the house, shut every curtain, and shut off most of the lights. As he struggled with the threadbare, rust-colored sofa, sweat pouring down his face, his mind wandered to the events of that afternoon.

April, Molly and Ms. Prescott were just leaving some rather somber meeting with Helen when he arrived to contemplate the mountain of paperwork he knew was waiting for him. The investigation had flooded his life with access requests and consent forms, and the strain of it was making him more tired than usual. He took his seat, barely noticing Helen, and began signing his life away to all manner of public officials when, suddenly, the air chilled, withered and died. Bellerose paid this no attention. His experiences with Helen had dulled his reactions to odd phenomena. Moments later, however, a series of dire coughs caught his attention, and he glanced in their direction to see Samuel holding Ellen aloft by her throat. He wore a long, black, leather coat and matching jeans, and in the artificial light, he looked paler still.

"Her blood for mine!" he cried, driving his long nails into her flesh. As dark blood ran down her throat, Bellerose took to his feet, and Helen's eyes widened in craven fear.

"She was promised time!" he cried, charging headlong at Samuel. "You cannot do this! MERI will...."

"MERI has already done its worst to me, old man. I do not fear the darkness as you do. This child has proven to be useless" he began choking her in earnest, "thus she shall be my revenge!"

The "old man" collided with Samuel at that moment but he might have taken more notice of a fly. His impossibly dark eyes were focused on Helen, who was kicking wildly and coughing blood.

"I...I...came here for h..her!" Bellerose cried, falling to his knees. Despite her agony, Helen craned her neck in surprise. "They'd taken her from me...said I could see her though...everything forgiven..." he sobbed heavily. "What do you want from me?" he groaned. "Are you after my research? I have lied for you, ruined lives, punished the innocent...my God, I killed a little girl! All I have ever asked for is the health of my daughter." Helen looked confused as her skin turned grayish blue.

"I'll surrender my findings!" he pleaded. "End my life! Only spare my Erin!" Grief seemed to be shaking his body apart. Struggling for air, Helen stared and felt pity for the first time. Samuel merely laughed.

"What you have done for MERI does not concern me. Nor does whatever research you might have "misplaced" while in their employ. Your daughter Erin has long been excised from this shell by methods even I might consider cruel." Helen's eyes were bulging in her head, and her mad struggles were beginning to slow.

"Erin is no longer, and soon, the same shall be said of Helen." He began shaking the suffocating girl like a rag doll while Bellerose bit into Samuel's leg. "Let it rest, Doctor." Samuel remarked, almost kindly, "She will die soon. You may weep. But know she will not be the last".

At last, the sofa blocked the door. Satisfied with his barricade, he cradled Helen's body, still bitterly weeping, and descended into a sparsely furnished basement. He whispered a prayer as he fell onto an ugly sofa. His heart anguished, he yielded to memory once more.

Five years ago he had been a thief and vagrant whose highest aim was escaping death. All work in his former profession had been closed to him, as had been any job that required even the slightest technical knowledge to perform. His former employers tracked him wherever he went, so he was quite mobile for his age. He cursed that moment of conscience, many years ago that had caused the downfall of his way of life. Dr. Allen Xavier Bellerose IV had been reduced to shoplifting to survive.

On that night, a merciless shower of freezing rain had beaten him further into the rat-infested alleys he called home than he had ever dared to go. He had been addressing the rodent problem in his mind when a huge crash captured his attention. Determined that he should sleep in relative safety, he snatched up a discarded beer bottle and moved stealthily toward the potential threat. What he saw appalled him.

Apparently abandoned there, a toddler of about four was crawling through the garbage. He glanced down at Helen's limp body through watery eyes, remembering how difficult it was to convince her he meant no harm.

"I'm sorry" he whispered miserably. "I ought to have let you alone."

"I will never forgive him!" It was evening now and Judith was starting to mend. Her voice was slowly returning to its full volume, the swelling in her legs was greatly reduced and it was clear she would be able to walk in a few days. The nosebleed had finally dried up and both eyes had regained their color. Most impressive of all, she was certain no nightmare would greet her this evening. But none of these small blessings concerned her. Her whole mind was consumed with a desire to make Alexander suffer.

The investigations against her aunt were due to end in two days and, as Ms. Wordsworth was always keen to remind Aries, the moment she was found guilty, she, Judith, would be shipped to the Virginia C. Wellheart Children's Center, and her last chance for a real family would die. Preliminary analyses by the Voice, Impartial, and local news stations were all bleak. Most opined that she should be in foster care already Her aunt's finances had become non-existent, and the very real possibility of hunger loomed ahead. She lay in her sickbed watching her aunt struggle to pretend everything was fine, and plotted grim revenges that she planned to carry out the instant she was well enough to return to school.

Her aunt was of similar mind. Judith meant the world to her. Ever since the day she had weathered a blizzard to be present for the birth, Aries had considered Judith her favorite relation. Since a dire tragedy in high school, Aries could not bear the thought of having her own children, so she had long considered Judith a daughter, and one of her only friends. She struggled with the bare hatred she felt for Alexander. After all, she was his teacher. She was supposed to understand and forgive. He could not have meant to bankrupt her and send Judith away. But as his image shone dimly on her television screen, she hoped for one horrible moment that they meant to announce his death.

"Good evening, ladies and gentlemen," a generic anchor was saying. "It's Wednesday September 26th, 1998 and you're watching WCSR-TV in Miriam. It's 7:30, and here's Dan Jennings with the news. The camera panned to a marble news desk surrounded by screens depicting wars, fires and other calamities.

"Thanks, Paul. Tonight's top stories: Local hero, Alexander Lightarrow, the brave child who exposed his teacher's abuse of her students, may be missing this evening. Police say they are looking into the matter but they believe it's to early to link this to the Sunrise investigation. In another Sunrise controversy, Vice-principal Allen Bellerose stands accused of strangling nine-year-old Helen Greywiche and barricading himself in his Salem's Point home. Police have him in custody. Finally, is Aries Washington guilty? Our panel of expe..."

She nearly broke the television as she angrily shut it off.

"Local hero!" she fumed. "He's a lovesick crybaby! And a liar!" She couldn't make herself feel the slightest pity for him, instead focusing that tender emotion on the fourth grader she had barely known. Then something horrible occurred to her Were Helen's death and Judith's attack related?

It made sense to her now. Prescott had been so calm because she knew Bellerose was on her side. Apparently, they both enjoyed abusing children. They, not she, had coerced the students into lying...and...and...April had forced Alexander to lie against her so she, April, wouldn't be forced to take the fall for Emma's actions. She thought she finally understood why those students that had worn the spirals had become organized. Bellerose had made them at once co-conspirators and victims. Her hatred evaporated at once, replaced by heavy guilt. She had to tell someone. She had to tell Alexander's mother. She had just reached the phone when there was an austere knock on her door.

Molly lay in her darkened room on a comfortable queen sized bed and cried bitterly. She had hoped the difficult trip to Contessa's would reveal some evidence that Alexander had escaped but after two hours of searching, hidden by a necklace containing some of Helen's mysterious power, she came to the agonizing conclusion that his was among the charred bodies still strewn everywhere.

She swore as loudly as she could without being overheard, and, when that failed to ease her grief, she began rhythmically banging her head against the bed's mountain of pillows. She just couldn't believe it. She had just seen him that morning chasing after a girl who was clearly too old for him.

"How can he be dead?" she wondered tearfully. At length, she simply cried herself to sleep, dreaming of the first time she had seen Alexander.

Ms. Leblanc's kindergarten class had been cold and quiet then. Molly had been labeled a nerd on her first day and abandoned accordingly. Because only a certain number of people could do an activity at once, she frequently had nothing to do. Arts and crafts as well as dolls and building blocks were always full by the time she arrived. As the weeks passed, she grew lonelier, until she finally started just falling asleep at playtime.

Then one day Alexander, melancholy even then, sat wordlessly before her and rolled a pink and white tennis sized ball. Ever since Aries, then a teaching assistant, had put them in their own little corner to play together and by the last day of class, Aries could never have imagined the pair ever being apart again. But the school's classroom assignments had separated then throughout first and second grade. They had reunited in Ms. Washington's class for a few happy weeks, and now he was gone forever. When Mr. Hall looked in on his daughter later he was startled to hear her whisper "come back" in her sleep.

Ellen was thoroughly exhausted. She had not been able to concentrate properly since Alexander's abduction, and she had only escaped Contessa's alive under his final protection. Escaping her rescuers without being carted off to the nearest hospital had been difficult, but the walk home had proved nearly impossible.

No longer able to make money as she needed it, Ellen was forced to make the journey on foot, and she could not remember all the lies she had told her parents to justify her late arrival. How she had escaped punishment was a mystery, but she was far more concerned with Alexander's whereabouts.

Tucked in bed, moonlight pouring through her window, she closed her eyes and softly whispered "where are you? Where are you Alexander?"

Over and over she chanted, concentrating harder than ever. Soon, threads of near light played through the darkness that was all she could see. These specters spiraled, shifted, spun and tumbled into a stream of light that looked like a prism. This melted into a puddle of light, rippled, and rose in great fountains to form, at last, an image.

By the light in her mind, Ellen beheld a tall, windowless building. Her eyes popped open excitedly. She knew where Samuel had gone. But Ellen was also certain that, if it came to it, she could not defeat the menace that had laid waste to Contessa's. Alexander's powers had shocked her, but they would not be enough. She would have to seek help. She shut her eyes.

Her child had been missing for less than twenty-four hours but Hannah was already out of her mind with worry. Where could Alexander be? A message on her answering machine informed her that he'd never shown up to school. She had been in a state of irrational panic before she had seen the evening news. Word of Helen's demise had driven her over the edge. She now stood before the Miriam Police Department desperately pounding the glass doors with her fists.
"Hel.....help me!" she wailed.
"Gone...Al...Alexander...gone....help!" Tears streamed down her face in boiling currents and her nose ran wildly but she couldn't care less. Presently, a thin, gray-haired man with a pinched face and keen eyes came to the door.
"Might I help you ma'am?" the man asked in a calm, slow voice. "I understand that something is bothering you, but we would appreciate it if you didn't burden the taxpayers with replacing our doors." He smiled. Hannah didn't.
"My son is lost! He never got to school....find...." The sentence was lost in a tsunami of tears. The man caught her gently by the arm and took her inside.
"Now then" he spoke, still calm, "have you a picture of the missing child?" he asked, and handed her a box of tissues. She nodded and produced one tearfully. She blew her nose violently as the gentleman inspected it closely. At length, he smiled. "Alexander M. Lightarrow, age eight. He was on the news earlier. We have several officers looking for him. I'm sure if you wait, they'll return any minute now. Hannah seemed to relax slightly. "Thank you, Mister...." "Detective Allen, ma'am, and you're quite welcome."

Ash County was home to several mysteries but none so dark as the secret hidden behind one of the exits of its interstate highway. The county shared a border with Virginia so traffic along the interstate never failed to impress. Remarkably few drivers ever discovered the false exit that led to a seeming dead end, but those unlucky explorers never returned.

Behind the dead end sprawled a shadowy tunnel whose entrance was guarded by a minefield, an automated laser array and several deadly snipers. The tunnel itself featured razor sharp glass shards embedded in the walls, machine gun nests, rocket launchers, a deadly poison mist and far fouler impediments. In addition to these protections, gray clad mercenaries stood at either end. Each of them had long ago lost any emotion they once held, and their motto had become "Shoot. Period." .

Beyond these protections lay a uniquely dismal city. The entire area was blanketed in a synthetic fog designed to block light, electronic intelligence gathering, and any and all outside signals. Wreathed in absolute darkness, tall, windowless, coal-black buildings sprouted up with military neatness. They had no apparent entrances and nothing, not even the smallest roach, moved in the streets. There had never existed in this realm any signs or other markings usual to a metropolis its size. The few that knew it existed had dubbed the city The Valley of the Shade, and lost within its bitter heart was the Mental Energy Research Institute.

The colossal skyscraper had no known history. The best explanation anyone could offer as to its present existence was that it had simply appeared where it stood around the early days of the Cold War. Since then, its occupants had carried out their duties in the direst secrecy. Few could explain the agency's purpose, and some could barely explain their own jobs. It was in this building, in a dimly lit boardroom some thirty floors up, that Judith now stood. She wore an exact replica of Samuel's white armor, and her box frames were missing. All of her various injuries seemed to have healed and as she stood there, arms at her sides, she looked both deadly and beautiful, like fire. Oak paneling sprawled around her but she paid it even less attention than the crimson carpeting beneath her feet.

Before her, eight austere gentlemen sat at an enormous, marble conference table. At its head stood a gaunt, snowy-haired Englishwoman in a black business suit, who wore such a terrible expression that her colleagues would not look upon her. She made a perfunctory gesture with her hand, and, at once, the men rose. She cleared her throat and spoke in an unsettling tone.

"I, Elizabeth Beatrix Stuart, fifth Director of Mental Energy Research, call this briefing to order." She repeated the gesture and took her seat. A moment later, the men followed suit.

"To begin" she began, "we will discuss the Project's problems. Valentine?" A corpulent, balding man whose battle-worn face was wreathed in white hair stood from his seat at the Director's immediate right, coughing violently.

"Project Sunrise" he said as his voice emerged from the coughs, "has been the latest installment in a series of policy directives aimed at controlling the ever-increasing strength of the Elements. The objective was to engineer, by means of psychological and behavioral control, an environment in which young Elements would turn to a false revolution to escape their misery. We also hoped to test the effects of Elemental powers in non-Elements, and whether our methods could achieve effective control of large populations." He was subdued by another fit of coughing.

"The "leader" of this supposed uprising, one Erin Bellerose was captured by staff four years previous and given the alternate personality "Helen Greywiche". She was instructed to engage her compatriots in a "revolution" against bullies and the teachers that inadvertently safeguarded them. In reality, she was to use her organization to deliver Alexander Lightarrow, an Element of unique ability, with no will to fight us, and whatever raw data..."

"Get on with it!" Stuart barked impatiently. Valentine nodded.

"Er, three problems exist. One, our former Society has interfered, kidnapping Lightarrow, and killing Greywiche, as well as several civilians. Two, the behavior of one of Greywiche's initiates threatens the mission. Three, the Ohiya, the device given Helen so that she might more effectively manage her ranks, has been unattended since her death. There is a possibility of it being found and used by unauthorized parties. " He sat down.

"Dawson!" Stuart ordered, turning to her left, "Solutions." Standing slowly he spoke in his groaning voice.

"The initiate in question will be convinced to admit her guilt, and the police will be discouraged from investigating further. As to Helen, Bellerose will take the fall. Things will quiet and we may end the project. As to the device, it has no power of its own without the presence of Elements. It should be the very least of our concerns. " He sat.

"And Samuel?" Valentine asked meekly, but Stuart ignored him.

"Begin at once!" she barked to Dawson, who darted from the conference room in great haste.

"Next" Stuart continued, glancing at Judith who remained still as stone, "we will discuss the future of the Element before us. Windsor..." But the liver-spotted near-hunchback was already on his feet.

"As you know" he yawned, "Miller was kidnapped and replaced with an alter on the night Samuel captured our target, Alexander. We have subdued her mind and are in control of her varied powers. The alter was designed years ago, as many of us expected something along these lines to occur. There are two courses we might pursue here. The popular choice is to send her after our primary target. With her abilities realized, she'd exceed Samuel's capabilities. Still, as he possesses Alexander, whose powers equal hers, I believe this an unwise strategy. Instead, I propose the new weapons be deployed, and she be trained as the fifth of that number."

As he sat, worriedly glancing at the Director's frown, Valentine opened his mouth to speak. Ignoring him, Stuart growled

"Originally, I meant to use her against the Society's remnant. Her superior abilities would certainly have ensured their demise. Since the Shade Project's completion, however, we have no need for her, or her kind. I have therefore decided she will be a test subject for our new weapons, the Shades. When testing is complete, we will eliminate every Element in existence, beginning with the Spiral Society, and those populating the city of Miriam. Dismissed."

The gentlemen rose and exited in unison, as the Director took one of Judith's limp hands in hers.

"You will die soon, little girl." she whispered. Still, Judith did not move.

Judith wept silently as she was led away. Police had taken in her aunt moments earlier amid dreadful currents of profanity that did nothing to make her look innocent. She was certain she would never be happy again, and every now and then, she pleaded with Ms. Wordsworth to let her return home.

"You'll be better off here" Wordsworth said for the hundredth time, as the oblong Children's Center came into view. "You'll be fed at least" she muttered, artfully braking the station wagon. As they approached the stoop and its heavy, red doors, Judith spied, through her tears, a little girl in a long, black shirt with fiery, red hair.

"Hello, Annabelle," Wordsworth called briskly as they drew closer. Judith saw the redhead rise from her perch, wearing a slight frown.

"Ann!" she called back. "Don't call me Annabelle. You know I hate that!" But Wordsworth seemed not to hear her, and the pair bustled into the Center, Ann in tow.

Inside the doors, a cool, quiet common room greeted them. It was afternoon, and the only light came through two huge doors at the back of the common room, which had been left open. A table placed in the left doorway joined one set up between the doors, and a few scattered members of staff reclined there comfortably. Beside the back doors stood a large cabinet, nearly buried in teddy bears, blankets, and other keepsakes. Carnations sat on a wicker table above a throw rug in the center of the room. The outside light shining on them made some of the petals grow. What looked like a tiny, pink dining table sat off to the side.

"Ah, Miss Miller!" a clever looking young woman exclaimed. "I am certain you are less than thrilled to be here, but try and remember that it may not be permanent, and make the best of things." The expression on Judith's face clearly said she had no intention of making the best of anything but she nodded slowly as Ann came up beside her.

"That is Mrs. Zevgolis, Judy. She's nice."

"Why thank you, dear!" Zevgolis smiled, patting the bun on her head, "Judy, if you will follow me please."

"Don't call me Judy" she answered quietly, but fell in lockstep.

Ann ran out the back door and toward the play area as quickly as possible, hoping to find her friend before Judith was done settling in. Her feet slammed heavily into the ground as she sought out her compatriot. In her excitement, she collided with a tall black girl in braids.

"Sorry, Elizabeth," Ann said hurriedly. "I was looking for Elizabeth." As she darted off, Elizabeth folded her arms and tapped her foot, openly laughing at her friend. Ann got as far as the Sleeping Quarters before she realized her mistake. Hitting her head, she trudged back to Elizabeth who was still laughing. Hysterically.

"What was all the hurry?" she asked when Ann finally ran up to her, panting desperately, "Keep running like that, little girl, and you'll break something you need" she giggled.

"I wanted to make sure" Ann coughed, looking annoyed, "that you remembered our rule! No "magic tricks", "feats of prestidigitation" or whatever you want to call it. We have to hide our powers or..."

"Or the boogie man'll get us. Right?" Elizabeth asked lightly. Ann gave her a cold look.

"I just think it's a stupid rule!" Elizabeth exclaimed, withering under the glare. "We have powers that let us have anything we want, but we never use them. Its ridiculous."

"But safe" Ann insisted stubbornly. Before Elizabeth could answer this, a gaggle of children came dancing into view.

"You win this time" she sighed. Ann smiled.

Life at Sunrise had become chaotic. The students should have been hard at work cutting jack-o-lanterns out of construction paper and baking witch shaped shortbread cookies. Ms. Washington should have been laughingly arguing with her students over how much sugar should go in the black and orange frosting. Streamers should have decorated the walls and ceiling, but this year, they did not.

Since Helen's murder, classes had thinned severely. Jonathan, Edwin, April, Bill and a girl named Carol had all been excused from classes by their parents. Even some teachers had refused to come to work. Much of the building seemed deserted. Worse, April had just confessed her guilt to reporters that morning citing the exact scenario Aries had reported to the press some time ago. In light of the investigation they hadn't believed her, but now, as Ms. Prescott joined Mr. Bellerose in jail, they bombarded the Principal's office with uncomfortable questions, all of which kept her from reining in the unbridled chaos that was developing. Worst of all, as Mrs. Ingrin, their substitute teacher, was learning, Helen's death left her acolytes free to run amuck.

Molly hit the floor beside her desk, narrowly avoiding a hail of chess pieces.

"You call yourself a teacher?" she shouted as checkers were fired back and forth. "I could do better!" Exasperation filled her face. Mrs. Ingrin deflected a well-aimed marble with her grade book and sighed. Moving to the blackboard, she scratched her fingers across the surface. A general outraged groan came in reply, and projectiles fell to the ground as several students rushed to cover their ears.

"Now I'd certainly appreciate getting paid to sit on my duff all day and watch you little monsters tear this place to ribbons, but I can't."

"You were doing just fine a minute ago!" a girl yelled out. She was ignored. "Therefore, all of you will clean up this mess, and then we'll begin learning."

"And if we refuse?" the girl asked dramatically, and her classmates waited excitedly for a response. To Molly's utter shock, the substitute had taken up a nearby yardstick.

"That's not teaching!" Molly yelled as her teacher swung the measure into the nearest group of students. They scattered before her, frantically gathering debris as they ran.
"See, it's working" Mrs. Ingrin remarked, and returned to her seat.

An hour later, Molly wasn't any happier. The substitute, determined to avoid work herself, had adopted Emma's silent reading approach to learning. Only the highly illegal threat of physical force was keeping open rebellion at bay. She was only pretending to read, however. Her thoughts were still with Alexander.

She had been relieved to discover that his guardian was certain that none of the bodies at Contessa's were his, but that meant that Alexander had been kidnapped, and she did not have the power to discover by whom.

"But April does" she thought sullenly.

Her best information indicated that the fire ants she had slipped into April's things had infested her house causing much discomfort and a small fortune in extermination fees. She had come to school in foul moods, covered in angry weals, and liberally cursing under her breath. When Molly thought about it, she hadn't stepped as much as paraded on her classmate's toes. The price for April's help, if there was one, would be steep, but she thought of Alexander silently rolling her the ball years ago, and realized she was willing to pay it.

Nearby, the same girl who had challenged their teacher earlier, one Carrie Price, slipped silently from her seat. Her hair, a lighthearted bubblegum pink, could be seen darting swiftly toward the yardstick that was keeping the class in line. As Molly observed, her stealth was unnecessary. Mrs. Ingrin had grown so bored with the assigned text, she seemed to have dozed off. The pink haired girl took up the weapon easily and stowed it behind the classroom's sink.

At once, the classroom erupted in whispers and general chaos began to brew. As the pink haired conspirator slunk toward the recently collected marbles, Molly made a decision, and slid out of her seat. She rubbed the necklace around her neck twice and hoped she had become invisible to the unaided eye. She was out of the classroom in a flash, but instead of taking the ramps, she turned left and stepped out through the side door. Three flights of stairs later, Molly was outside and diving, unseen, toward the Rainer residence about nine blocks away.

She was partway there when she bumped into a still weepy Ellen Lockett. Highly agitated, the older girl had barely noticed the collision, and she kept her march up doggedly, until Molly's apologies reached her ears. Instantly, dislike warmed Ellen's body. She had wondered how Ms. Prescott had discovered them at Arcadia Park ever since Alexander caught a glimpse of her, and they had both hidden along the path they had come by.

"It must have been you!" Ellen thought bitterly. "You snitched so you could have him to yourself!" Molly's feelings for Alexander were well known to Ellen. April whispered about them frequently as a means of snaring the young target. Ellen resumed walking, angrily now, determined to find Alexander and thwart Molly's hopes. But she hadn't taken two steps when she was caught about the arm. Molly had different ideas.

"Let me go!" Ellen demanded harshly, but Molly shook her head.

"You saw him last" she sputtered. "Where has Alexander gone?"

"I don't know!" Ellen lied. "Now let me go or you'll..." But Molly wasn't listening.

"Tell me where! Please!" she begged. "I know you used your powers to find out! You were going to him now, weren't you? I swear I'll follo....no!" Molly wailed.

Ellen had very quietly whispered "Elysium", and vanished in a ripple of air. Overcome with anger and sorrow, Molly cried openly, staring at the spot where Ellen had been.

"Heartless little brat!" she screamed into the slight breeze. Still veiled in Helen's charm, she waited there for almost an hour, hoping for some sign of Ellen. When the girl did not return, Molly sighed, and sullenly plodded towards April's home.

A small, shrub bordered walkway told her she had arrived at her destination. It was a large, white, house that bore a brass knocker shaped like two turtledoves. The rightmost dove was missing a wing, and though that diminished the knocker's beauty, it had never been repaired. Clasping the cold brass timidly, she knocked twice in quick succession , and tapped the necklace again. Mr. Rainer had none of his daughter's powers, and would never have seen Molly otherwise. But her knocks had been too light, and no answer came. She tried again, with more force, and almost at once, the door flew open...and was slammed in her face a second later.

Before she could knock again, the door opened once more to reveal a tall, blond haired gentleman in slacks and a pressed shirt, whose pointed beard and round eyeglasses made him look scholarly.

"You are Molly Robin Hall correct?" he asked jovially. She nodded. "Ah, I did think so!" the gentleman cried lightly. "My daughter claims you are responsible for the recent rise in our fire ant population" he remarked, as he ushered her inside. "No need to apologize!" he sang, waving away her fevered stammerings. "These are yours, are they not?" he asked, handing her a pile of notebooks. She nodded slowly. "Then there's no need to apologize." he repeated, smiling. "You've come about the little boy, haven't you?"

"Does she tell him everything?" Molly thought, blushing. Out loud, she spoke hurriedly. "I wondered if...ouch!" A fire ant had crawled up one of her sneakers and bitten her ankle.

"That's what you get!" April shouted, diving up the crimson-carpeted staircase to their right. Mr. Rainer sighed good-naturedly.

"I doubt you'll get anything out of her" he remarked. "Stubborn as a mule, that one. Still, I've always said one good theft deserves another." At precisely that moment, a scream issued from the second floor.

"Where's my diary?" April cried furiously.

Laughing, Mr. Rainer shoved a pink journal atop the notebooks Molly carried. She looked shocked.

"Run for it!" he chuckled, holding open the door. "She'll realize any minute now." Amazed that April's father would release his daughter's diary to a stranger, Molly scampered out the offered exit spouting many words of thanks.

"It's nothing!" the jovial man called after her. "My daughter's a brat!" The moment she could no longer see the house, she dropped her notebooks and began skimming the diary.

"Where is he?"

The gentle sound of weeping echoed in the forest clearing. High in the trees, birds sang woefully to one another as they sailed from perch to perch. They seemed to share the pain of the creature below. Kneeling in the sun-kissed grass, Samuel wept quietly, thinking of what he had seen there some days ago.

Samuel, like most of MERI's Elements, had been captured as a child. He'd been twelve then, living in a quiet Virginia suburb. His father had died some time ago, but life with his mother was comfortable and easy. Nothing adventurous ever happened, and everyone was happy to keep it that way. Then came Mitsy.

Odine County had never seen anything like her. Wild and willful, she had none of the slow, conservative mannerisms of the area. She brought chaos and adventure where they had never been before, and Samuel loved her for it. He was the only one. The rest of the town found her wild hairstyles and spirited greetings offensive. Unnecessary contact with "that crazy girl", as she was known, was socially forbidden, and that ruling led to a massive argument.

It began one evening when Samuel's mother heard, through various gossips, that her son and "Manic Mitsy" had kissed. When Samuel returned, his mother grabbed him by the shoulders to explain "social standing" and "civilized behavior" but the love struck kid heard none of it. Since his mother meant to keep him from Mitsy, he ran away from home. Somewhere in the darkness of Odine that night, a hand had slipped round his throat.

"Mitsy stays alive only if you do as ordered!" he remembered hearing, and from that day forth, he had.

Then one day he came to the clearing, the only place he was allowed to see his love, and found blood gushing from her heart. He wept more bitterly as he remembered it, and anger coursed through him. He had looked around for her assailant for several minutes before something appeared, seemingly out of thin air. It wore an impossibly black cloak that seemed to be alive, and an imposing suit of lightweight black armor. It had no face, just a smooth head that looked as if it were made of black opal. The air around it quivered and grew unbearably humid so that Samuel's skin began to feel leathery as she suffered a crippling migraine. Trees began to splinter along their barks as Mitsy clutched her chest painfully and fell to her knees.

Enraged, he foolishly attacked. Shutting one eye, he concentrated inward, and momentarily, the skin on his fist seemed to fissure, revealing patches of extremely bright light. Soon his entire fist shone like the sun. He leapt at his foe, the light flaring to resemble a sword's blade, and deftly aimed where its heart should be. But almost more quickly than his eyes could follow, its cloak blocked the strike, and at that moment, the very air caught fire, and Mitsy was clasped in flame. A moment later, the sky began to fade into darkness as crimson streaks of sunlight braided together and barreled toward the earth. Mitsy had long ago burned to ashes that sailed within the firestorm, and now the deadly fire closed in around him. Then the earth moved and everything went white.

Samuel continued his anguished crying as the memories came to him. He had obeyed their every order without question. So why had Mitsy been killed? He had left his mother, and his home, and become death's right hand, all for Mitsy, and still she had been killed. MERI had betrayed him, and the blood of hundreds was on his hands. The small revenge he had taken was not enough.

"I will punish their entire city" he whispered. His lungs began to burn then, as a cloud of white dust engulfed the clearing. The instant it touched the trees, they crumbled into piles of ash. The birds and other animals became a fine dust that rained down about Samuel. The very earth grew dry and cracked. Samuel began choking as the fine sand tore at his lungs. He couldn't say a word, and soon, blood poured from his mouth. He shut his eyes against the violent storm, but he knew what was coming. Sure enough, he soon faced the thing that killed his first love. Beside it stood the Director of Mental Energy Research.

"There shall be no more kidnappings, for I have declared war on your kind. I no longer have need of any of you. Our past mistakes will be rectified!"

The thing beside her closed its fist tightly and a beam of sunlight fell like lightning, piercing Samuel's back. A second beam struck his head, and the First War was begun.

Chapter Four: The Spiral Society

"Lights, please" a voice echoed in the darkness. At once fluorescent light filled the small room. A small, white examination room came into view. A hospital bed stood against the wall, and the door directly before it was bolted shut. A kindly looking young doctor with crinkled black hair considered the near-dead mass the bed was supporting.

"Poor little thing" she whispered. Amazingly, it began to stir, and when it tried to raise its head, the doctor clearly saw the badly bruised face of Alexander, the child MERI had recovered several days ago. "He's still alive!" she thought with wonder. "Can you hear me?" she asked calmly. He gave a brief shudder she took to be an affirmative.

"I am Dr. Yasmine James" she began more firmly. "When you are able, you will refer to me as Dr. James. You were captured by Samuel, a former member of the Spiral Society, and this life, and submitted to tortures aimed at eliciting your obedience." She considered the wide burn than ran down his spine, obscuring the spiral Helen had placed there.

"You were then recovered by us following his death, and you will have to be put to death unless I can convince the Director of your usefulness. Therefore, I intend to court your loyalties by more scientific means. If you wish to live at all, you will cooperate. Do not fight me or you will perish. Is this understood?" Another shudder gave her the impression that it was.

She examined her patient closely. Alexander wore only his underwear, and thus, a wide collection of burns, bruises and scars were clearly visible. Dr. James shook her head.

"Primitive" she remarked.

Fetching supplies from the cabinets behind her, she checked his blood pressure, heartbeat and pulse, all of which indicated he was in stellar health, despite what her eyes told her.

108

After confirming this with more complex tests, treating his injuries, and wedging Alexander in a hospital gown, she felt it was time to begin more serious business.

"This will not hurt in the slightest." she stated, as she sterilized a devilish looking needle. If Alexander had the energy within him, he would certainly have protested. As it was, he gave a third shiver, and moments later, the upper area of his right arm was injected with a liquid that resembled quicksilver.

"Tiny machines are being introduced into your blood." Dr James explained. "Though these, and the accompanying drug, I will be able to directly affect your thought processes. If you don't struggle, this will all be over soon."

With a powerful hallucinogen clouding his mind, Alexander found it difficult to think, let alone resist. "Perhaps you will live after all" the doctor thought hopefully.

Several floors below them, in what looked like a large, padded gym room, the Director sat in a balcony at the far end, protected by indestructible glass. Below her, a young, black scientist stood wearing a gleeful look. All of his features stood at neat, ordered angles, and his eyes shone vividly in the room's white light. Dr. Xavier Almos Talbot, MERI's best scientist, had reason to be proud. It was his invention that would, at last, lead the Institute to glory.

"Madam Director" he began. "two years ago, I refined the distillate from the remnants of the Rulix crystal, an artifact we recovered around the time of the Great War, and concentrated the energy within it beyond previous parameters using semisynthesis. Combining the resulting liquid with chemicals derived from ergot, I created a psychoactive substance of immense usefulness with a threshold dosage level of the order of 20 to 30 micrograms. Trials revealed a variant of hyperflexia wherein patients displayed, in addition to overactive reflexes, increased speed and agility in movement. Several types of synesthesia were also reported, but I weeded out all but one, wherein patients hearing a particular rhythm, as in a simple rhyme, would involuntarily adopt a personality devoid of emotion. Sill more interesting, paresthesia occurred to the point where the subjects were unable to feel pain at all, no matter how severe. Finally, a brief euphoria as the drug's effects begin to show seemed to ,forever after, cause the affected mind to associate well being with obedience to the administrating official. I named my invention Abiteth and increased the dose in future trials.

The new dose opened the subject's mind to suggestion, and in moments, not weeks or months, but moments, their wills were thoroughly destroyed. Significant mutations began to be observed, most of which were not viable. In the four that survived, I noted heightened sensory awareness, though all the necessary apparatus seemed to have vanished. We have been testing my creations, called Shades, for some time, and as I have insisted since their initial completion, these beings, who in addition to being infused with distillate have their right forearm embedded with crystal fragments, are capable of wiping out the Society and should be released at once. "

Dr. Talbot gazed confidently at his Director. He felt he had made his case, and indeed, Stuart looked mildly impressed. She found the microphone beside her and ordered,

"Show me, then. An Element stands before you. You will order the Shade you have brought here to destroy it. Do not fail." Talbot laughed heartily.

"I couldn't possibly". Turning to the Shade that stood beside him, he ordered, "Attack the Element" in a calm voice.

At once, the creature turned to face Judith, who wore armor nearly identical to the type Samuel had worn at Contessa's. Talbot quickly exited the arena by one of its heavy, titanium doors, and reappeared moments later at a respectful distance from Stuart. Seemingly unfeeling, Judith rose into the air like a marionette and pointed her right palm at the Shade's forehead. Six thin beams of blue light emanated from the cardinal points of her hand, forming a marble sized ball between her lifelines. A second later, a deadly beam tore toward the dark thing below, but it simply vanished, reappearing a second later behind his attacker.

He caught her by the throat and viciously hurled her to the ground. Palpable darkness began to spread over everything, and no amount of glass could halt the pinched, choking feeling that consumed scientist and Director alike. Little by little, existence seemed to be ending. Light, breath, thought... all of it seemed to crumble in the spreading darkness. Skin drew painfully tight, and bones felt as if they were being powdered. Talbot could not make his lips form the command that would save them. There was a crimson flash of light and the room seemed to explode, but the darkness drew ever tighter. Then, suddenly, it was gone, and reality crept back.

Judith stood up, blood gushing down a broken arm, and began a new attack. Leaping at the Shade, she closed her fist tightly, and what looked like a searing rain of meteors began to pelt it mercilessly. It phased into darkness and seemed to flow backwards on the nonexistent wind.

"Why are we still alive?" the Director gasped suddenly. Fear lined every inch of her face as she shakily regained her composure.

"Judith distracted the Shade somehow" Talbot explained. "My guess is by not dying."

The Director's reply was lost in the horrendous peals of thunder that suddenly broke out. Lightning tore across the room, shredding Judith's hail, and a swift kick between flashes sent the poor girl sailing into the leftmost wall.

Blood sprayed from Judith's mouth, accompanied by a few teeth. If she could have wondered at this point, she might have wondered why she wasn't in agonizing pain. As it was, she freed herself from the wall and charged her foe, two fierce waves of golden energy coursing along beside her. When she came within range, she slashed her hand forward and several crescent blades of energy tore toward the Shade with ridiculous speed. But such efforts were in vain.

The cloak leapt in the way, absorbing the damage, and strengthening the powerful bolt of lightning that slammed through Judith's skull the next moment. The child fell, the battle ended, and the Shades were prepared for release.

Aries had no idea that her real niece had died in a secret city of eternal night. Despite April's testimony, Miriam police were unwilling to release her, or return Judith. So the former teacher remained a "guest" of the Sacred Light Behavioral Institute, which she believed to be a fancy name for "loony bin with more bars". Grant Jeremiah Hastings, a sharp-eyed black man known for his sleek dreads and empathic disposition, had mercifully replaced Ms. Wordsworth. Unlike his predecessor, he visited frequently, and was determined to see mother and aunt reunited once more.

"Now the police are stalling because this new information makes it looks like they didn't do their jobs, and they don't want to consider it if it can be avoided. Now, unfortunately, it can be." Hastings remarked. "What I can do" he continued, "is stir up a bit of trouble for them. I'll go over their heads and force them to present whatever flimsy evidence they have against you in light of the girl's confession. If it isn't sufficient, I can demand your release, and when you are financially stable, the return of your child."

That sounded wonderful to Aries but she stretched forlornly, and lay on her cot.

"You're gonna convince'em that Aries, The Crazy Woman, Washington is sane, huh?" she asked. Hastings nodded resolutely.

"Shouldn't be that difficult, actually. The girl claims to have coerced the children, and that the adults were silenced by Bellerose. If he confesses, or the children are convincing enough, some action will have to be taken."

"I'll bet Amanda's taking action!" Aries grunted sarcastically.

The Principal of the scandal-ridden elementary school hated to be wrong. Worse, she couldn't tolerate the idea that child abuse had occurred under her nose without her ever noticing. Thus, she was sticking to April's lie, and quietly silencing dissent within her thinning ranks via extra work, trivial detentions, and more strenuous classes. She had justified her actions as in the school's best interests, but Aries wasn't buying.

"She cannot keep them all quiet" Hastings replied calmly. "Someone will talk soon enough." Aries frowned.

"Soon enough can't possibly come soon enough!" Aries exclaimed. Hastings nodded.

"I apologize" he said, rising, "but I must tend to another client now.

Two floors above Ms. Washington, in minimum security, Hannah Bennett wept into her cot. She was heavily sedated, and under the sharp eyesight of three nurses. Miriam's finest had never recovered Alexander,, and it had driven her crazy. Bricks had been hurled through Aries' windows, and impromptu visits to Sunrise had been made. When she began to rave wildly at her fellow nurses she had been subdued in a most efficient manner, brought to her current resting place, and placed under Hastings' counsel.

"Unless you've found him go away!" she groaned miserably. Used to this form of greeting by now, he sat at the foot of the cot and sighed.

"We'll find him soon. I'm certain of it" he said hollowly. "And when we do, you must be in good condition to care for him. That means..."

"Yeah, yeah" Hannah interrupted. "Sane. I know. No more howling about that kidnapping b.."

"I just visited her, and she gives me the impression she's innocent" Hastings interjected quickly.

"Does she now?" Hannah asked bitterly. "Well pop your head back in there and see if she gives you an impression of where Alexander is." Hastings sighed.

"Prescott and Bellerose are more likely to know the answer to that. The police are questioning them, and so will I."

She laughed cruelly, but seemed mollified, though it may just have been the effect of the sedatives. Whatever the cause, Hannah soon fell silent, and Hastings turned to leave.

Thanksgiving was fast approaching, but Judith couldn't think of anything she was thankful for. She missed her aunt painfully, hated Alexander bitterly, and still had no friends. Sure, Ann and Elizabeth came to her rescue whenever her compatriots threatened her safety, but Ann was just as moody as she was, and Elizabeth was much too cheerful. Mrs. Zevgolis was indeed nice. In fact, Judith got the feeling the woman was coddling her. She felt trapped in a fog of gloom, and recently, uncertainty. Sometimes she felt as if she were a character in a book someone was reading. As if she were looking down at an illustration of herself. Her memories were becoming less solid. Increasingly, she became obsessed with the idea of being reunited with her aunt.

"It'll all make sense then" she told herself.

Almost immediately, a tennis ball made contact with the back of her head.

"Say you're sorry!" an indignant voice rang out behind her and, seconds later, Elizabeth came into view, her round face pinched with the effort of pinning a little boy's arms behind his back.

"Never!" he called out defiantly. "You can't make me!" And with a clever twist of his arms, he freed himself, scooped up the tennis ball, and hurled it at Judith.

"Stupid girls!" he crowed, leaping out of reach, and he dashed across the play area with all possible speed.

"I can't stand that kid!" Elizabeth complained, taking Judith's hand. "If I could only use my powers" she thought to herself. She looked about surreptitiously, and found Ann almost at once. "Darn" she whispered sourly. "That just leaves the hard way. Judith?" she asked suddenly, "How fast can you run?" Elizabeth smiled darkly.

By the time Mrs. Zevgolis came to the rescue, the poor boy was suffering a monstrous wedgie at Elizabeth's hands while Judith administered a fierce wrist burn. Ann and a few others had shown up and were laughing heartily at the kid's struggles. He remained unrepentant.

"I'll kill you when I get out of this!" he screamed, to general amusement.

"Then perhaps I should leave you here" Zevgolis interjected, detaching Judith from the elastic of his underwear. "But I will not" she finished, freeing his wrist. "Now what's all this silliness about?" By the time the story was told, Judith felt slightly better. As the boy was marched toward time out, she smiled properly for the first time in ages.

There was no joy at Miriam's Dreamland amusement park that day. The park was only six or seven years old but its roller coasters and Ferris wheels attracted large crowds. Unfortunately for that number, nine of these were Elements.

The sky above began to grow dark as noon fell. The winds fell still, and a woman vomited. Throats roared with pain and coughing, eyes swelled, skin grew ashen, and people wasted away in plain sight. The metal beams supporting the rides rusted in seconds, and their burdens crashed to the earth. Fire and the wails of death consumed the land as those still able tried to drag their mangled forms to safety, but it was all in vain. The last thing one little boy ever saw was a cloaked shadow strolling through the flames.

The blaze grew exponentially. Eventually, it was spotted by the local fire department. It took sixteen hours of work to subdue.

"The hell happened here" one fireman was heard to comment.

"We're dying!" a blond haired woman cried, enraged. "They don't care anymore! Playgrounds, theme parks... they blew up a church yesterday. A church!" she screamed, almost hysterically. "Their weapons are horrible. Worse than we ever were. We're going to have to take a stand!"

A general grumble of assent filled the shack they were hidden in.

"And how" asked a gaunt fourteen year-old with dingy hair and sandy stubble pock marking his face, "are we to do that? Samuel, our leader, is dead. So are most of our members. And the Institute's killing Elements to extinction. And that's just been three of those new Shades. How are just two dozen of us..."

"We don't have time for this!" a nine year-old exclaimed suddenly. "We've got to run, Dismal. We can't beat these things."

The fourteen year old stared into the crude fireplace and its cold ashes. "Nicholas is right" he agreed. "We can't win. Let's run."

"And let them kill as they please? Is that your plan, Judas?" The gaunt young man shook his head.

"No, Dismal. I would fight if we had a chance, but we do not. They have made their promised "ne plus ultra" and there is no surviving it." A quiet young schemer stroked his long nose and asked "What if we had the two kids that escaped a year or two ago? Their powers never did seem natural. Maybe they're stronger than usual." Dismal shook her head.

"I destroyed their entire neighborhood. Killed their parents...friends..." she stared thoughtfully at nothing.

"True" the schemer replied. "But the Shades will do far worse if they will not fight. Tell them that, and they will join us. " Nicholas looked livid.

"Two more Elements won't save us!" he yelled. "We'd need an army. There aren't that many of us le..." His words were halted when a look of incredible greed spread across Dismal's face.

"I have an idea" she chuckled.

These were the last remnants of the Spiral Society, a class of soldiers who, until Stuart came to MERI, were considered to be the ultimate defense against rouge Elements and, by association, anarchy. They were unlike many other fighting forces in that they were respected as something more than heroes. Whatever a loyal Society member requested would be seen to, even before the needs of the Director. Because their function was so critical to MERI's success, a lot of care was taken to secure their happiness. It was an effort of singular difficulty.

Nearly all of the Elements who made up its ranks were coerced into doing so by the Society itself. Their methods included torture and destruction. Often, entire villages were sacrificed for the sake of a few Elements. By the time most joined, they were homeless, parent less, friendless and loveless. It never took much to acclimate them to the task required, but unhappiness often led to rebellion.

When Stuart came, as Deputy Director, she became suspicious of the Society at once. Even with all their training, they showed too much emotion for her liking. Samuel, in particular, was a concern of hers. She influenced her Director, Dr. Cadmus Forester, to turn away from the Society whenever possible. When she became Director herself, her first directive was aimed at replacing the Society. Now her plans had been realized at last, and the world was collapsing around the remaining Society members.

"Now remember" Dorothy said, smiling sweetly at Alexander, "only the Good Witch can lead you to Oz, and home." Alexander nodded. He'd been skipping down the yellow brick road for three weeks now, but he never felt happier than when Dorothy spoke to him. The walking was easy, and his steps were light, for each one brought the Good Witch closer. And, as Dorothy constantly reminded him, that was the only way home.

117

Dr. James considered her work with pride. All of her tests showed her patient's mind was starting to yield. A week ago, Alexander had stopped questioning her orders altogether. He would be reliable, she was sure, long before Christmas, when she planned to make him a present for the Director.

On a nearby wall, a screen that resembled an overlarge poster showed her what the child thought he was seeing. A small square in the lover right corner showed his brain activity. She stared at her program for a minute, then decided to add something new.

"Run Progress Log." she ordered. The image before her shifted.

"Record all you see so the Good Witch can help us." Dorothy explained, handing Alexander a journal and pen. "Now remember, only the Good Witch can lead you to Oz, and home." Alexander nodded and began to write.

"Very good" the doctor laughed, checking the implant behind his right ear. "Now you've no time to think."

"You must report exactly what you write!" she heard Dorothy cry. "And we must follow the yellow brick road. If we leave it, the Good Witch won't help us. Now remember..." The doctor simply smiled.

So far, her efforts had somehow gone undetected. According to all MERI records, Alexander had died via lethal injection some time ago. Dr. James had falsified those reports in order to complete her experiments. She hoped to refine her methods of control such that they could bring even the most problematic minds into conformity more rapidly than anything else. Rumors of a silent war had reached her ears, and if she hurried, her efforts would guarantee her promotion.

"Work quickly, Dorothy" she mumbled to herself.

The diary lay open beneath a puddle of light. Molly had poured over its pages for weeks. The more she read, the more she hated April. But she hadn't located a single clue as to where

Alexander might be. She had desperately sought Ellen at her home, Sunrise, and everywhere in Miriam she could reach, but the elusive little girl remained out of sight. Finally, she had turned to anyone with any of Helen's powers, but none of her former compatriots would help her. Instead, they teased her mercilessly.

So she sat at her desk poring over the diary, hoping she had missed something, though she knew she hadn't. Halfway through the messy pages, she came upon a picture of Alexander she had seen more than a dozen times before. It was bound to the page by invisible tape, and showed the boy staring into the sky.

"He never saw it coming!!!" April had scrawled beside it. The page or so that followed showed April relishing the beating she had delivered. Molly growled in hatred and flipped to the last pages.

"Helen's really upset about something" Molly read. She was surprised. Few people were brave enough to refer to Helen by name. "It doesn't matter" she thought, and read on. "Really, upset. But it doesn't matter. I've grown tired of doing things her way. At recess, when he joins us, I will keep him instead of surrendering him to Helen. She says he is as powerful as her so he can help me take over. She's definitely hiding something. If I could only find the Metal Eye..."

"What's the Metal Eye?" Molly asked herself for the hundredth time. April referred to it several times, but never explicitly said what it was or what Helen used it for. Molly had been trying to guess via context clues for some time now. All she knew was that it was somewhere in Bellerose's office.

"It must have something to do with Helen's powers if April wants it." she thought to herself. Then she felt a shock. What if April already had it? Dropping the diary, she dashed for the front door and was neatly caught at the collar by George Alawishus Hall.

Reedy and plain, with cropped brown hair and spectacles, there was no question that this was Molly's father. Mild mannered but unusually clever, as fathers went, he smiled down at his catch and said the word Molly hated most in the world.

"Dishes, sweetheart. You've neglected them for far too long." She gave him a plaintive look.

"Not now" she begged. "Later. Please, it's really impor..." He shook his head.

"It's been three days now, Molly" he said gently. "There's no one else here anymore, so you have to do your chores, and I have to do mine. You cannot leave until then. Understood?" Sighing deeply, she nodded and rolled up the sleeves of the plain, white shirt she was wearing.

Twenty minutes later, she dashed down Weeping Willow Lane at top speed, not stopping once till she reached Sunrise's doors. Touching her necklace, she became invisible to normal eyes, and crept through the school she'd been truant from for some time. Now came the tricky part. She had to wait five minutes for a teacher to come out of the office so she could sneak in without making it look as if the door was opening itself. Once inside, she had to climb over scattered boxes, crawl around untidy furniture, and avoid bumping into anyone to reach the Vice Principal's office in the rear. She was three steps from her goal when the adjacent door opened, and Ms. Phillips exited, deeply agitated.

"They're still asking far too many questions" she grumbled to herself. "If they keep this up, there won't be a Sunrise Elementary much longer."

"Perhaps you should stop hiding the truth then" a passing, hassled-looking secretary said.

"For the hundredth time Bea" Phillips replied I'm not..."

"Yes, you ARE!" came the sharp reply. "Kids in detention for no reason just so they don't squeal is hiding..."

"I will not let this school be shut down!" Phillips shouted. "Not for a little girl and a teacher who won't take responsibility for what they did. Not because some kids chose to run away..."

"What about the murder? Huh?" Bea snapped. Molly saw her Principal's face burn bright red.

"The old man's nails weren't sharp enough to do the damage and the fingerprints around Helen's neck weren't his."

"The police still have him, though" Bea observed.

But Molly didn't care any longer. She dived, unnoticed, into Bellerose's office and began silently searching the desk. Clearly, she was not the first. Each drawer revealed chaotic tangles of paper, pencils, folders, notes and other trinkets that had been brushed aside in the search for evidence. She combed through these carefully, and after two hours, discovered a strip of paper that featured tiny, shaky handwriting. It read

"Ohiya. Speak at the mirror and behold my power."

At once, Molly searched the room and found a small, square mirror lying on a file cabinet. Clasping the looking glass, she gazed into herself and called out "Ohiya!" From that moment forth, Molly never looked in a mirror again.

Her heart pinched painfully as the darkness within it came into view. All her anger with April, her growing hatred of Ellen, it all splashed in torrents of raw pain. Her teeth ground against each other as the glass rippled and bled upon itself, at last revealing a small, ashen white medallion depicting a golden braid encircling a silver triangle in the center of which was a dim, crimson eye. Shakily, she placed the thing around her neck, and at once, its purpose was clear. She had no power of her own, but she could take it from others as she pleased. Feeling zombified, she tucked the thing under her shirt, and prepared, at last, to find Alexander.

Bellerose had long decided that whoever had captured him, it wasn't the police. Imprisoned, handcuffed, and bleeding in several places, not a single question about Helen had greeted his ears. Instead his tormentors seemed to only be interested in his research.

"Where have you hidden it, old man?" a sharp voice asked. "Why won't you simply talk?"

"Because when you have it, you will kill me" Bellerose groaned. Coming into view, Dismal nodded.

"True. But if you cooperate, I shall do so far more quickly, and with significantly less pain." A foot slammed into his hand.

Elizabeth awoke with a start as the glass on the windowpane cracked and shattered. It had taken some time to find the place, and the exact people who could help her, but Ellen had arrived at last. Elizabeth leapt from her bed, looking like an archangel in her long nightgown, and caught the young intruder by the throat.

"You better tell me who you are quick!" she growled, "Cause they'll never find your body if you don't."

Ellen was frightened to say the least. Her journey had been a long one marked by distractions, indecision, and a deep pity for the people her disappearance would drive insane. And now she was struggling to breathe while staring into the loveless eyes of one of the people her powers had shown her.

"Ellen!" Ellen gulped desperately, "My name is Ellen Lockett. I know you have powers, and I need your help." Elizabeth released her grip only slightly.

"How do you know about my powers?" she asked harshly. Ellen related her varied adventures at Sunrise, her encounter with Samuel, and Alexander's capture.

"I just want Alexander back" Ellen finished, as Elizabeth released her.

The other girls began to awaken, and Ellen quickly shut her eyes. At once, the glass repaired itself, and when the girls saw only what appeared to be the commonplace occurrence of a new arrival, they regained sleep with startling efficiency. All except Ann who had caught her friend's eye.

When Ann had heard the story, she began crying quietly. She opened the window, and the three slipped away.

Her bare feet were tickled by the cold blades of grass as the group scurried toward the entrance to the Children's Center. Her face still streaked with tears, she dashed toward an unknown city, and dreamt of a horrible past. She had been five years old then, and as anyone will attest, that is an inglorious time for the world to end. She and Elizabeth had just met some weeks ago on the kindergarten playground at Sunrise, and they had become fast friends. They had been innocent then, living in a world without powers, sorrows, or death. Their parents had loved them; teachers pinched their cheeks and tickled their tummies. Friends told them they could be anything they wanted in the whole world. But then, one balmy, quiet night, fire had rained from the sky.

At first Ann had thought the brightly lit sky and the streams of flame that fell like shooting stars to be pretty, and she had watched intently. But soon, walls of screaming tore at her ears. Her little corner of Miriam exploded into flames, and a moment later, her mother kicked in the door. Thick, black smoke billowed in after her.

"Cover your nose and mouth, Ann!" she screamed as she snatched up her daughter and charged back through the door. Ann heard her mother coughing bitterly as smoke infested the woman's lungs.

"I can walk!" Ann insisted, struggling to regain her feet so her mother could crawl beneath the haze. But Ann's mother held her still more tightly, and dived down the steps. Plumes of fire rose about them but the woman pressed on, now running on pure instinct. At the bottom, she let Ann down to tear open the front door, but the moment it was open, a katana lodged itself in her throat.

Ann shrieked and smoke entered her lungs as the door fell back and a cloud of fire exploded into the room. Her mother collapsed, wreathed in flame and spurting blood, and Ann's plangent wails echoed through the blaze.

Ann fell to her knees, soaking with tears, and waited for death to come. Greedily, the flames devoured everything around her until she was encircled. Sweating profusely, she groaned "Mommy!" over and over, weeping horribly.

Suddenly a blood-soaked blade broke the ring of flame, held by a woman in white, metal armor. Blond hair flew in all directions as the cold looking figure approached, skin glowing in the firelight. Ann nearly roasted herself trying to escape. The woman placed the tip of the blade at Ann's throat, and some of the blood stained the child's clothing.

"Annabelle Rachael Morning!" the woman's voice boomed austerely. "You will kneel and serve me henceforth, or I will rip out your..." But further threat proved unnecessary. Among the burning ashes of her home, she knelt tearfully. The woman swept Ann crudely under one arm and walked back through the conflagration.

Ann began to sob as she remembered her mother and all the dire terrors that had befallen since her murder. Presently, a warm hand rested lovingly on her right shoulder and Ann turned slowly to met the tear-filled eyes of her closest friend.

"We'll stop them" Elizabeth sighed heavily, "so her friend won't end up like our parents."

On Monday November 30, 1998, the city of Miriam suffered through its worst day in over three decades. Faced with the scandals at Sunrise, Helen's murder, a rising number of violent incidents, and several missing children, Miriam had already been at a fever pitch. Authorities had decided that April's confession was authentic, and that Principal Phillips, who by all reports was censoring anyone who hadn't followed her lead in discrediting it, had played a role in the child abuse scandal they believed they had uncovered. She was arrested that morning, and the school was to be closed after the remaining students left in the afternoon.

Some parents had arrived to protest the closing as, for many, Sunrise was their child's only option. Clarence Elder, the school's bony custodian, was cleaning out the atrium near the fourth grade classrooms one last time, when he heard a jarring noise, followed by a scream. Three stories below, a blond-haired woman stood at the head of a group of two dozen. In her arms was a half dead old man whose research, she had discovered, was useless to her.

Her compatriots produced semi-automatic weapons and corralled the protesting parents in the All Purpose Room. Along with Bellerose, they were bound, gagged and placed in groups at the lunch tables. When the prisoners were settled in, Dismal indicated four of her crew.

"You watch these fools and make certain they don't move." She led the remainder up the ramps, and toward the classrooms.

The captives were surprised when their monitors almost instantly abandoned their weapons. Encouraged, one old man began to struggle with his bonds. Turning to face him, a pale fourteen year old in faded jeans pointed two fingers at him. At once, a golden beam tore through the air and left a neat hole in the man's shoe. Muffled gasps of surprise filled the room, but no one moved after that.

"Well done, Judas!" cried a rakish young woman in a "Swift Detectives" tee shirt. "Now if you'll all remain still, no one else will be hurt."

"And if you believe that, there's a bridge in San Francisco I'd like to sell you" Nicholas mumbled quietly.

"What was that?" she asked, facing him.

"Nothing, Maeva" he replied quickly. Experience had taught him that upsetting the brown-haired beauty he was forced to work with was unwise.

When Mrs. Ingrin's door flew open, she did a pathetic job of pretending she hadn't been sleeping at her desk. Nine students remained in her care, all of which had once worked for Helen. They stopped in the middle of the controlled chaos they had been creating to look upon their guest.

Blond and tall, Bertram clapped his hands twice, and the class was suddenly frozen in place. Smiling darkly, he simply motioned for them to follow and, like marionettes, they obeyed.

The substitute trod after them, rubbing sleep from her eyes, and received a sturdy kick to the shins for her efforts. In short order, Dismal's forces returned, new captives in tow.

"We have them all!" Bertram reported smugly. "Every Element at Sunrise."

Chapter Five: The Grim Revolt

The last fragments of the Spiral Society, once near holy in the eyes of their masters, paced through the All-Purpose Room monitoring hostages. The mysterious golden beam still fresh in their minds, no one offered resistance, though some quietly wept. One member of the tearful minority received a rude shock when a patroller took her chin in his hand, a rather hungry look in his eye. A pale redhead of coldest beauty, Alice Rexler gazed at the cruelly sharpened smile of Icarus Grentin, aged fifteen, with daggers in her eyes.

"I could be your mother!" she thought as she tried to shake her chin free. She was backhanded for her efforts.

"That will do!" Dismal asserted, taking the stage. "Play later. We have work to do."

Looking like a spoiled child deprived of chocolate, Icarus stole a rough kiss before returning to his duties. Alice's eyes narrowed murderously.

Dismal had donned the white armor of the Spiral Society and as she prepared to speak, she looked somehow more human than she had in over a decade. Ignoring the microphone completely, she simply spoke, her voice seeming to fill the room.

"My name" she began, "is Emilie Malinda Terrwyn, though most simply call me Dismal. We have captured you today to resolve a complicated situation. As Judas tells me you've seen, we have powers your government has secretly used countless times for their benefit. We were captured as children, and tortured until we followed orders. They had us kill or capture anyone like us so they could keep our powers under control. You're here because they don't need us anymore. All the recent mysterious "accidents" lately were attempts on our lives. All of them successful. We're here to put a stop to that" she said looking at the children.

"If your child isn't bound and gagged beside you, he or she is an Element and has powers like we do. All of you children will use those powers to fight alongside us."

Quoth Carrie Price, "Never in life."

Dismal waved her hand. Nearby, an old man started choking painfully. Beside him, a woman started coughing blood. Panic spread as more and more people broke into violent illness.

"All right, all right!" the girl shouted feverishly, and in the echoes of her sentiment, the coughing died.

"Secure the building!" she ordered her patrollers, "I'll initiate these Elements. We will need more of them to have any chance of survival."

"They're not like us, the people here." Dorothy opined. "They're very tricky folk, always trying to take you off the road. You have to ignore them. Just listen to me instead. I'm the only one you can trust."

Dr. James monitored the tubes that fed Alexander intravenously. By stealth and uncommon cunning, she had obtained a syringe of Abiteth, which she injected into Alexander's right arm.

"My methods aren't working rapidly enough" she mumbled to herself. "You will bring chaos, Alexander. Chaos that I control. Then I will bring order. I will outshine him at last. And you will live."

She monitored his vital signs and adjusted her equipment as necessary.

"I have twenty-four days left." She was still determined to finish by Christmas.

She had been passed over too many times. The Director back burnered any idea she came up with, and it irritated her to no end. Talbot was MERI's star. Whatever he said seemed to stand. But Dr. James had Dorothy working night and day, and soon, all that would change.

128

In MERI's conference room the following afternoon, Winston Valentine had no concerns for his career. His thoughts were focused on living through the conversation he was having.

"So, the remnant of the Society has gathered at the Sunrise Elementary School in Miriam, pressed everyone Helen gave power into their service, and taken the rest as hostages. They've secured all entrances and exits, and there's little means of eliminating them without Miriam knowing, as the building is surrounded by police and journalists." Stuart slammed her fist into the table.

"Kill them! I don't care how. All any sort of diplomacy will achieve is time for those insects to find any Elements I haven't already killed. When this was begun, we wanted a weapon for ourselves, and only ourselves. One we could control. And now that weapon is complete. Time to terminate the failures."

Valentine nodded, and quickly left.

At that moment, a chilling, unfamiliar sound filled the air. The plaintive notes were from air raid sirens that rang throughout the shadowed city. Bursts of gunfire sounded between them.

"Some hapless driver has found us" Stuart laughed, continuing to mull over her plans.

Outside, a submachine gun fell to the earth in two halves. Sniper fire ripped deep holes in the ground, which shook unnaturally, forcing three guards to their knees.

"Hurry!" Ann shouted as she dived into the tunnel. At once, crimson lasers, a wall of bullets and a massive explosive force enveloped her. A flash of white light filled the enclosure, and Elizabeth and Ellen heard the thunderous roar of still more mines exploding. Donning the same shields of light Ann had just summoned, they dived after her with inhuman speed. Moments later, they rocketed out of the far end, pursued by a massive wall of flame. The guards raised their weapons and prepared to fire, but were instantly engulfed.

Breathing heavily, they each focused until their eyes shone like the sun at dawn. The city sprawled before them, clear as day, though its dark veil remained unbroken.

"Stay together!" Elizabeth warned. "They'll remember the last time." At her words, Ann shook badly, glancing high into the air.

"The last time" had been three years ago. As they dodged the lasers that suddenly rained upon them, Elizabeth remembered the scent of lilac wafting through a room many would have thought elegant. A royal blue and gold pattern bloomed on the carpet beneath two pearl white love seats, which faced each other, and the sofa between them. Everything was trimmed in a rich, gilded wood. A glass coffee table sat in the center, and beside the love seat on the left, an elegant end table supported a stunning lamp. A dazzling chandelier hung above the coffee table, and was reflected in the mirror on the wall behind the sofa. It was the most extravagant room in the entire Valley, but to Elizabeth, it was the entrance to a prison.

Beyond the splendor of the Briefing Room, sixty-six stories above ground, those Elements who had been tortured into seeing the light were trained, fed, rested and kept happy enough to kill others without attempting to kill their masters. On that day, Inverness, the headquarters of the Spiral Society, had been her home for three years. By the time she arrived, it had already been nicknamed the Castle in the Air. No one had ever managed to escape its walls.

"In line at once!" Samuel had greeted them that morning. She, Ann and dozens of others had dutifully fallen in a neat line, one beside the other. No one wanted to discover what the punishment of the day was. Staring arrogantly at his soldiers, Samuel consulted a sheet of legal paper.

"Today we will be eliminating seven Elements, ages 9, 12,7,5,8,6 and 11, near Weeping Willow Lane. All destruction will be explained to the government as the work of the elusive Desert Rose and his agents. Do not pity these less than human things, but kill them by any and all means."

130

They all nodded, and followed Samuel into the night of the city, when Elizabeth, snatched by impulse, grabbed Ann's arm and dove into the sky. In her time with the Society, she and Ann had murdered 73 people between them, burned large sections of Miriam, and tortured new recruits. They'd cried themselves to sleep for a year and a half, but now the work was becoming far too easy.

"What are you doing?" Ann yelled in shock as they winged toward the sky. But Elizabeth was too busy concentrating to answer. Samuel followed them that very instant, calling hail and lightning from the sky.

"If they escape, their punishments are yours!" he called below. Instantly, a dozen golden beams fired around Elizabeth. But she had enshrouded herself in a blinding white light by then and they bounced off uselessly. But the roar of each lightning strike was ringing in her ears and dodging the hail and Samuel was becoming difficult. In addition, others had taken to the air in their own bids for freedom.

Growling madly, Samuel lunged through the air and ripped Ann from Elizabeth's grip.

"Run away!" the redhead screamed. Instead, Elizabeth stopped concentrating, and fell like a stone. Her entire body weight slammed into Samuel, dislodging Ann who took off like a shot. Seconds later, Elizabeth joined her.

"You've finally lost it!" Ann panted, dodging a volley of beams from the less hopeful. "It'd take a miracle to get us out of here!"

Elizabeth shielded herself in light just as a hail of sleek, arrow shaped micro missiles exploded around her.

"The Judgment Arc!" Ann screamed, indicating a weapon perched atop the shadowy buildings below. It looked like someone crossed a Vulcan cannon with an English longbow. Machinery in the bow shaped areas constantly loaded missiles into the twelve barreled cannon. Ann shielded herself in time, but two young Elements behind her weren't so lucky.

The revenant returned to earth at the sight of their compatriots' mangled flesh, leaving Samuel to focus his attack. Choking fire, piercing lightning, and falling stone filled the skies, along with golden beams fired in earnest, and winging higher was becoming impossible. And Samuel came ever closer.

"Disobedience is death!" he called, adding two huge plumes of fire to the chaos. Ann's hair exploded in flames just as they reached Shamayim, the layer of signal blocking cloud. Elizabeth flew to her friend at top speed and, grabbing her, screamed "Nova!"

The world went white.

Elizabeth shivered as her memories came through the darkness, but despite their daring invasion, no further resistance barred the path to their former prison. Ellen gazed at the massive skyscraper for the first time and knew a spreading sense of dread. Only knowing that Alexander was inside gave her enough courage to ask "how do we get in?" As they floated toward the quay on the sixty-sixth floor, Dr. Yasmine James saw her chance.

She had given Alexander far more than a threshold dose of Talbot's drug, and already, the changes had taken firm hold. His hair and face had long disappeared. His skin was the color of pitch, and the texture of stone. A gray cape flowed from his shoulders, a living appendage, and now, he was covered in plating. All that morning she had tested him, and found Dorothy's work was flawless. He would obey her and only her henceforth. Somewhere within, anger burned. She had still needed Talbot's help. But she would recapture the escaped Elements, and her time would come.

The girls arrived at a blind door hidden in the west wall of the sixty-sixth story.

"Simsim!" Elizabeth cried, placing her hand against the cold, dark, wall. The next moment, she wished she hadn't.

A wide, dingy hangar met their eyes. Its walls were badly dented and spangled with dry blood. Many of the lights that dotted the ceiling were badly broken, and a horribly unbearable smell brought them all to tears.

"Dear God!" Ellen exclaimed. Piled carelessly in the center of the unlit room were at least two dozen dust-cloaked skeletons clearly belonging to their former compatriots. Rats scuttled to and fro, and they knew at once that they hadn't always been mere bones. Several showed deliberate breaks or were hopelessly twisted. Elizabeth was filled with profound guilt.

"Their punishments are yours" she remembered painfully. "Disobedience is death." They had been killed in retaliation for her escape. A brittle, papery, sesame flower lay undisturbed nearby.

Full of tears and struggling not to vomit, the trio made for the dim hallway that led to the Briefing Room, careful not to disturb anything. Scattered bones and blood littered the area. Clearly, someone had tried to escape.

"Simsim" Ann whispered as they reached a second blind door. The Briefing Room was unchanged except for a thick layer of dust that covered everything. They passed through it quickly as well as two rooms full of basic beds, and file cabinets, to arrive at the central hall of the MIRI building.

"Alexander?" Ellen breathed wishfully as they walked down the hall. There was no carpet, no pictures, nothing of the slightest comfort. She shuddered as they turned the corner and ran into Dr. James, who wore a victorious smile. Alexander stood beside her, though he barely recognized himself.

"Shade number five" the doctor commanded calmly. "Capture the intruders."

Detective Christopher James Allen stood on the threshold of Sunrise Elementary School with bags in his eyes. Three children were missing, one was dead, and now he was mediating a hostage situation. No demands, no way in, and no escape from the media. It was the twenty-first, and if he didn't figure this out soon, his grandchildren would have to get along without him for Christmas.

As he mulled the situation over, is thoughts strayed, as they often did in tough times, to his former partner, Peter Lightarrow. Back when they were a team, he remembered, this particular assignment would have been much simpler. After all, Peter hadn't been called the Hellfighter for no reason. Detective Allen had to laugh as he pictured his partner beside him, saying, "*you* negotiate. I'ma go in the back way".

"I will find Alexander, my friend," he thought soberly, and focused his mind on the task before him

Inside, Dismal had different problems. Food supplies for her prisoners were running low, and sneaking new Elements past Allen was growing difficult.

"Nosy old man" she thought, swearing under her breath as she paced through the All-Purpose Room. Four times already Allen's crew had nearly found a way past her defenses. Only the continued use of her powers kept the police at bay.

Meanwhile, the hostages were proving to be far more trouble than they were worth. She had long ago replaced their binds with cuffs and shackles so that meals and bathroom breaks required less supervision but none of it was easing the strain. Many times she had to struggle to keep from slaughtering them all and having done with it. But they needed more time, and more Elements if there could be any chance for their survival, and the hostages kept Miriam's eyes on Sunrise. Stuart would find secret action difficult.

Rumors had come to her, via freshly captured Elements, that Stuart's city had been invaded, and a battle raged. One that was growing increasingly one sided. These whisperings were confirmed when three members of the Society placed Ann, Elizabeth and Ellen at Dismal's feet. Broken and bloody, the girls had run for their lives, and were grateful to be prisoners, rather than dead, but now, in addition to everything else, Dismal had to cope with Ellen's incessant weeping.

134

"Shut up!" the captor hollered. "He's dead most likely. And we'll die too if you don't concentrate on healing."

"I don't care!" Ellen bawled, but before Dismal could reply, Elizabeth dashed tipsily for the door.

"What is with you and escaping?" Ann called as Dismal caught the runaway by the hair.

"I'm not killing anyone else!" Elizabeth spat still spangled with numerous bruises. "And that monster knows we're here. It'll come…"

"Of course it's coming!" Dismal screamed. "Why else would I be doing this? They'll find us wherever we run so we have to fight. Now stop running off!" With that, she threw Elizabeth to the ground.

Beneath them, in Miriam's dank sewers, three Shades moved with inhuman speed. An Eloapis, a hovering platform seemingly made of stone, bore Elvin Davenport, a hard-faced young man, behind them. He questioned whether leading three deadly weapons underground was covered by his job description as Dr. James's assistant. Mere moments from now, they would be underneath Sunrise Elementary School and Stuart's desires would at last be achieved. The Elements would fall, the United States would finally have at its disposal the most powerful weapons in human history, and the credit would go to Dr. James.

"Let's hope this "take over the world" scheme works" he mumbled, and pressed on toward certain victory. As Allen stood outside gleaning answers, and Dismal paced inside, playing for time, Alexander coasted at the head of his new brethren, splattered with the blood of his former friends.

Chapter Six: The Battle at Sunrise

"How dare her!" Stuart growled glancing at several flashing monitors. "How did she get them to follow her orders?" MERI had been in disarray all that morning as James' creation, revealed at last, repelled the girls' ill-fated rescue attempt. In a rage at the boldness of the Society, she had planned to launch a Shade at Sunrise, the closest thing they had to a stronghold. But her monitors indicated that Dr. James had launched three. Two were MERI's but the third was different. Clearly it was somehow allowing James to command the other two.

"I will make her pay as soon as she's finished doing my work for me" Stuart mumbled. Seconds later, Talbot rushed into the Monitor Room flushed in anger.

As the Shades drew nearer, Bellerose let his mind wander somewhere it had not in a long time. Susan Hallows had been one of Helen's friends and an early adopter of her plans. His hands quivered as he remembered her struggles beneath the pillow. When he left MERI, he had sworn never to harm a child again. He tried to make Helen change her mind, but he had been consumed with thoughts of Erin for some reason, and couldn't properly concentrate. Then the screaming began.

Like April, Susan had the sensation she was falling into a dark pit of nothing and screamed loudly and without pause, until Allen was sure his eardrums would burst. He had slammed the pillow on her face to silence her, not aid in Helen's brutal punishments.

"One more thing to pay for" he thought miserably, "when these people finally kill me."

The air rippled then and Dismal looked up, alert, until a dust laden child fell to the ground. Clearly famished, threadbare, and weak, Molly crawled into a sitting position, angered that Ellen could see her like this.

"He's coming" she sputtered weakly. "He's coming now" she repeated, and fainted. Ellen stared at her, pity mixing with hate. And then fire consumed her world once more.

The floor tore like paper as the Shades exploded into view. Flames raced around the walls in currents. A moment later, the room began to boil, and a fine dust invaded everyone's lungs. Ann screamed as it tore Bellerose and anyone else without the Rulix crystal's powers apart. Elizabeth tried to talk, but her lungs were much too busy combating the invading dust. Protected by the grim powers of the medallion she still wore, Molly arose painfully and delivered the first volley.

She sacrificed all of the power she had stolen for her search for Alexander to send a razor-sharp bean of light into the chest of the nearest Shade. The attack was swallowed by the creature's cape as Molly fell out of consciousness again. A second later, waves of light filled the room as Ann charged toward Alexander.

"Death before surrender!" she cried, striking him hard with a glowing fist. The dust bore down, and the fire raged on.

Hannah Bennett watched in anguish as Sunrise Elementary collapsed on the television above her. She had been pretending for days to understand that Alexander might never return to her, but seeing his school in flames, after all the other accidents she had heard about was more than she could bear. Weeping loudly, she changed the channel, and prayed that wherever her son was, it wasn't there. The nurses had yet to fall for Hannah's ruse, and she wasn't going anywhere for some time. On the screen two blond haired young girls in trench coats were laughingly solving mysteries.

At Sunrise, Allen, the fire department, and the National Guard tore their way inside. The television crews stayed a safe distance away as plumes of flame tore the school apart. Inside, Ann screamed inconsolably as memories of flame and murder filled her mind. Beside her, Dismal launched her foot into the face of the nearest Shade and dived into the air. Seeing Ann, a look of disgust clouded her face.

"First Ellen, now this" she murmured. "You'll end up like your mother thaaaaOUCH!!" Dismal screamed, falling to the earth. There was a deep hole in her left arm. Ann shot by her, somersaulting into the air, and slamming her foot into another Shade's head.

Every now and then, a pulse of light shot from beneath the smoke. There, struggling to breathe and remain conscious, Molly fought her way to safety. But it felt as if the Ohiya she wore was killing her. A huge weight seemed to sit over her heart, and her skin felt as if it had been drawn tight. Her thoughts, as always these days, were rooted firmly on Alexander. As the roaring flame began to weaken the floor she ran as fast as possible toward the room's wide doors meaning to escape and find him. The powers she had stolen told her he was here somewhere, and she refused to leave without him.

Behind her, Ann screamed chillingly as she swung a crescent of light into Alexander, her hair blazing fiercely.

"Ann!" Elizabeth screamed, as a cold fist slammed into her jaw. Plumes of water cascaded over Ann, soaking her to the skin, as Elizabeth plunged into the thick smoke below. In a flash, Ann raced after her, gripping aimlessly in the shadows until she caught Elizabeth's arm. When they cleared the smoke once more, Ann was nearly bald, and sported wide burns.

"Thanks…" Elizabeth coughed.

"Ditto" Ann replied weakly.

Elvin Davenport returned the way they had come, seeing no need to be burned alive for the cause. He figured he had done all Dr. James needed to, "and if I haven't she can do it herself for all I care." He was certain the Shads would be recovered, and he sailed away with all deliberate speed. Behind him, still trapped within the All-Purpose Room, the Elements that remained alive were of similar mind.

"Can we escape now?" Elizabeth asked weakly, as two more Elements fell beside then. Ann nodded and they crawled toward the exit. But smoke could not hide them from the Shades. Bolts of lightning rained around them at once, and one Shade shifted into a black cloud of sand and flew toward the door with remarkable speed, becoming solid just in time to slam a foot in Molly's head and halt her advance. Her nose began to bleed.

"They're not gonna let us leave!" Dismal spat. She swore loudly as Nicholas was flung into her injured arm, but the gaping hole in his chest silenced her protests. Dismal had been far removed from pity for some time. Her work had hardened her heart against the sorrow of death many times over but at that moment it briefly flared in her eyes.

Oxygen in the room was, by now, non-existent, and the four story school building was seconds from collapse. Ellen crawled through the flames, her lungs screaming for air, and took hold of Ann and Elizabeth's ankles just as Alexander reduced the floor to splinters. Blood poured from her lips as she cried "Elysium", and the world became white.

"You're watching the Evening Report on WCSR-TV. Preliminary reports on the fire at Sunrise indicate that it was a terrorist plot carried out by an American cell of the Bloodied Saints, an illegal organization led by the so called "Desert Rose". Police believe the Saints are also responsible for the string of "accidents" that have recently plagued Miriam. Police estimate at least thirty people died, many of whom were children, and the historic elementary school, the first to be integrated in our state, has been reduced to smoke and ash in the worst attack on American soil since Pearl Harbor. "

Behind the anchor, cameras panned over the smoldering bricks and piles of rubble that once comprised Sunrise Elementary School. Though several weeks had passed, smoke still billowed from the once proud institution, and none could offer any explanation. Stragglers hung near the edge of the ruin weeping bitterly, and mumbling about funeral services.

"A vigil will be…"

Aries shut off the television, glad for the first time that Judith had been placed in foster care. She was free now, but until she found a new teaching job, she could not have custody of

Judith. She still had no idea of the fate of her little girl. She couldn't possibly know the innocent that was attempting to console a panicked Mrs. Zevgolis at that very moment was an imposter.

Zevgolis had lost her mind some time ago and the Evening Report wasn't helping. The Center had seen its share of runaways, but they usually came home within the hour. It had been some three weeks now. Thanks to Dismal's actions, there was little to be done about it.

"Couldn't you call the police?" Judith suggested stubbornly for the ninth time. Zevgolis sighed.

"I've been told, in no uncertain terms mind you, that the Miriam Police Department is far too busy investigating the fire at the school to look for foster children."

A moment later, she put Judith and the other kids to bed, and spent the pale December night pacing through her quarters.

The frigid wind dancing across her broken flesh, Dismal dragged an unconscious Molly into the depths of a dust-laden cave on the edge of Virginia. Tears and dried blood stained a face that was cradled with haphazard shocks of now ashen hair.

"Nicholas" she mumbled morosely, and she stopped to take the broken little girl in her arms. "Why'd you take this thing?" Dismal asked herself, jangling the medallion around Molly's neck. "False power's all it is."

She wasn't sure how she had eluded the Shades, or why she insisted on wasting energy rescuing Molly. All she was certain of was that the thought of a world without Nicholas brought tears to her eyes. Sparing his life had been her last act of kindness in living memory, and that notion frightened her. So hiding often and trusting no one, they had trekked for some time to arrive at this cave, a place of safety according to what little power she had left. She laid the girl down on a large, smooth stone, and at once, her head exploded with pain. Thick drops of blood ran into her left ear as a well-thrown rock fell to the ground.

140

"For my mom" breathed Ann, groaning heavily. Beside her lay Elizabeth and Ellen, who were no better.

To weak to fight, they collapsed near each other, the final survivors of MERI's first purge. Their thoughts and motives varied, but persecution had brought them together. Presumed dead for the moment, they at last had some measure of freedom, and in their haze of pain and anger, this became clear. Their first battle had been badly lost, and it would be weeks, if not months, before some of their wounds healed. Above that, nothing could remedy Dismal's brutal murder of Ann and Elizabeth's parents. Soon, they were certain, their wounds would heal, and their grievances would take hold once more, but for the moment, they were unlikely sisters in a common destiny.

Beyond their improvised shelter, Miriam suffered on. Drowning in loss, fear and sorrow, the community began to languish and abdicate its power. Christmas came and went, amid somber, tear-ridden tidings, and the New Year crept upon the city like a lecherous drunk. No shouts of joy, peals of laughter, or songs of innocence greeted travelers to Miriam on the first of January. Instead, the entire city was draped in the melancholic silence of death.

Behind a certain false exit, however, Stuart wore a cruel smile, perhaps the only one in the city. She sat in the glass box of her Exhibition Room, dreaming of future success. Below her, Dr. James scurried at top speed, positively insane with fear. She felt the air about her grow unbearably hot, and fell to the floor, weeping hysterically. Passers by heard dense thuds and cracking noises that they had learned to ignore completely. But Dr. Talbot stopped to listen, his expression one of heartless glee.

Despite a bombed out tunnel and a few dead guards, the Valley of the Shade remained untouched. As blood splattered the padded gymnasium floor, Elizabeth mulled over her plans for the city.

Extra Chronicle One

The Redeemer's Tale

Daniel had never been like other children. While his friends might have concerned themselves with games of baseball, the latest music, and elementary school romance, he was shut up in his room, always, lost in a book much larger than any his compatriots had ever seen. It was a small room with a wide, round window that let sunlight spill upon the writing desk before it. Perched atop a sprawling mansion, it showed the world a clear distinction: Daniel was rich and, unlike his fellows, he could not come out to play.

Daniel's parents, the Rivulets, were owners of what many black people called "the world's strongest bank". Established during Reconstruction, the Absolution Bank of Maryland had weathered segregation, war, depression and near financial collapse through a series of clever strategies and unexplained miracles. Like all its previous owners, Virgil Rivulet had inherited the responsibility of its operation the second his studies were ended, and he continued to keep the bank profitable using his father's reinvestment techniques. It was these his son, Daniel, now studied so ardently.

Ever since his eighth birthday a few days ago, all hope of relaxation had ended. His father had taken him aside to explain that they "lived in a cruel world". Virgil had been immovable on the point that neither the Bank, nor all the money it generated, would earn him the respect of the people he would meet.

"You can depend on only two things in this world" he asserted. "God and your own mind."

His best friend, Aries, had stopped calling on him soon after that. She spent the last days of summer wondering why Daniel chose to read at his window when the first day of school fast approached. But ice cream and soda pop dulled these thoughts magnificently and, despite Daniel's absence, her last free days were glorious.

The night of September 3rd, 1954 would be forever burned into Daniel's consciousness. On that night, just as he started to nod off in the middle of his studies, three sharp knocks came at the door. Three fierce, arrogant knocks. They were answered by Geoffrey Ward, the house steward. The open door revealed a gaunt man with fierce eyes cast deep in a furrowed, puffy face. He wore an austere gray suit, loafers the color of ash and a pair of steel frame glasses that made his eyes all the more difficult to bear.

"Are you Virgil Anthony Rivulet?" asked a dry, bitter voice. "I have a matter of some importance to discuss."

"And whom" Ward asked stiffly, should I say is calling?" He folded his hands together. "At this hour" he mumbled to himself. "With no appointmen..."

"Never mind all that!" the man griped harshly. "You are obviously not the person I have come for. Fetch him, and you may say that Dr. Leeland Harper III is calling." He said this last sarcastically.

Dr. Harper was the chairman of the Board of Education for the state of Maryland. Recent national events had made it his job to enforce the integration of Miriam's public schools, a move he had opposed for years. He seriously doubted his associates would understand that his hands were tied so he had personally come to exercise the luxury of hope. Several minutes later, Virgil appeared at his door in a crimson smoking jacket made of velvet and trimmed in silk satin. His slacks were off-white and seemed to be made of similar materials, and he wore a wine red pare of suede shoes. Tall, broad-shouldered, and elegantly bald, Virgil had the rough look of someone who had acquired his wealth and knowledge by dire labors. His neatly trimmed beard and moustache gave him a look of fierce intellect. His greeting was not warm.

"Sir, it is late, and I was in a state of rest. In future, you might show more consideration for..."

"Listen, Rivulet." Harper barked suddenly. "Money won't solve the problems you'll have if you fail to manage your tone in..."

"Do not threaten me in this place." Virgil ordered firmly, as Mr. Ward allowed Harper inside.

"Why have you come to "Little Africa" as you have called it?"

Swallowing his anger at the gall of his host, he crossed the rich, royal blue and white carpet of the living area, and sat in one of the luxuriously cushioned straight-backed chair there. He marveled at the Rivulet's wealth. Recessed lights in the gold leaf concave ceiling gave the room a mystic aura. In the ceiling's center, a massive chandelier draped with fascinating beads drew his eyes. Between the chairs and on either side of them stood round, white, marble tables. A thin vase that held seven white lilies sat on the center one. The side tables featured elegantly designed lamps. Starlight poured in through the huge, richly draped windows behind him. Immediately before him stood a mahogany coffee table. To the left of this was a crimson, velveteen love seat and to its right, a matching sofa.

"How's he doing it" Harper thought enviously, "if a respected citizen of Miriam, like me, can't afford half as much?"

When he had taken it all in, and Virgil sat in the chair beside him, Harper spoke as calmly as he could.

"I am here, Rivulet..." "That's Mister Rivulet" Virgil interrupted, "just as you are Dr. Harper."

"Fine *Mr*. Rivulet" he spat venomously, "I am here to convince you to see reason. Tomorrow, the new school year begins and for the first time, I am obligated to force schools to accept members of dissimilar races."

"No problem there" Virgil intoned coolly.

"That's where you're wrong." Harper replied. "The fairer population of our state will try to prevent it by any means, which may mean danger for you, your wife, Patricia, or your son. In

144

addition, my colleagues in government will bear down on myself and others to become stricter with you people. Naturally, their first target would be "the world's strongest bank". Why suffer needlessly?"

"I simply choose to, Dr. Harper" Virgil replied coldly. "I will not prevent my son from attending the only schools for which you will authorize funds in this state. I will say this, however. Patricia and Daniel are precious to me. What harm is given to them will be returned a thousand fold, and damn the consequences. Now if that is all you have..."

"There is more!" he cried viciously. Harper slammed his fist on the center table so hard, the vase nearly fell from its perch. "If you wake Patricia, you will regret it!" Virgil whispered fiercely.

At that moment, the house steward approached.

"Sir, Master Daniel has asked me to investigate the source of a recent loud noise, and I am quite curious myself. Your wife remains asleep, but I suppose she would be curious if a similar sound should awaken her."

Virgil turned to his steward.

"And what was Daniel doing when you left him, Mr. Ward?" he asked calmly.

"Analyzing methods for the continued financial stability of the Bank" came the answer.

"Very well" Virgil replied. "Tell my son he may retire for the evening, and that our guest became a bit impassioned. And make certain Patricia is not disturbed."

Ward nodded, and was gone.

"I need you to speak against this, Virgil" Harper said the instant Ward was out of earshot. . "The others will listen to you. I am prepared to pay..." But Virgil held up his hand for silence.

"I will do no such thing, Leeland." Here, the doctor frowned, but kept his peace. "These are times of great opportunity for all of us, and I will take no part in halting that. Now please leave." Harper stood violently.

"Fool!" he rasped. "There is no opportunity to be had. You will help me tonight, or face an angry mob come morning." Virgil marched to the door and held it open.

"Get out!" he growled evenly, and Harper made for the offered exit.

That had been one year ago. As Harper had predicted, Daniel and the six other students chosen as the first black children to be educated at Sunrise Elementary School had suffered through mobs, threats and violence. For the first six months, President Eisenhower ordered the Maryland National Guard, which was doing very little in the way of discouraging violence, under Federal control. During that time, six US Marshals, derisively nicknamed "The Zookeepers", kept them from being beaten, kidnapped, or worse.

But things had calmed since then, and the neighborhood's children had long grown tired of the controversy, so these days, Daniel sat at his desk in relative peace, thinking up solutions to the problems his new environment had exposed him to. Beside him, Aries scribbled notes at a frightful pace. Her long, crinkled auburn hair had attracted a lot of attention from the boys in the class, but she paid little attention to them. Instead, she focused on Dorabella Fieldswallow, the vibrant lady with a crown of blond hair who had agreed to teach them.

Unfortunately, she had not promised to be polite, and quite often, made no attempt at it.

"Those of you who are capable of reading please help everyone else find page thirty-seven in our text. Text means book" she finished, staring directly at Daniel. One smart aleck attempted to show Julian Roberts, another of the seven, the relevant page and nearly lost a finger in the process.

"Now then" she continued, before we begin, can anyone tell me who James Madison was?

"This ought to be good!" she thought when Daniel raised his hand.

"Go ahead, boy" she said out loud, and was thoroughly surprised to hear his answer.

"James Madison Jr. was one of the most influential Founding Fathers, the principal author of the Constitution, and the fourth President of the United States. He also owned slaves."

"Thank you" Dorabella replied dismissively, and launched into her lecture.

At recess, Aries found Daniel drawing in the dirt. She saw what looked like a simple map of Weeping Willow Lane, a struggling community to the west of his home. Every few inches, there were large rectangles, and a series of what looked like mathematic equations lined the picture closely.

"What on Earth is that?" she laughed kindly. "It looks like a map. Looking for treasure?"

Smiling, Daniel shook his head. "This is Weeping Willow Lane. I've got a plan to improve the whole area for free!" Aries sat in the grass beside Daniel giving him a look that said "you've got to be kidding."

"It's simple!" he began. "We volunteer on weekends to pick up all the stray bits of trash, and tell the adults to petition for trash cans at each of these rectangles so that trashing things properly becomes more convenient. The cleaner walkways will attract business and..."

"And shouldn't we be playing?" Aries asked. "You stayed inside for most of the summer. So now it's time to have fun."

"But I want to do something important" he replied, returning to his map.

"Fine" Aries laughed, "let's go integrate the sliding board." Daniel laughed at that, and ran toward the playground equipment, Aries in tow.

Three years passed, and Kevin Fieldswallow, Dorabella's eldest son, was not enjoying his firs duty as an officer of the law. He stood upon a huge stage erected on the grounds of the Miriam

Public Library, just off Weeping Willow, and prepared to affix a medal to Daniel's chest. When it was fastened, he did the same to Aries, Julian, and Crystal Hope, the only white child on stage. When the medals were pinned, Dr. Harper took the microphone and spoke in tomes that hid his true feelings.

"Citizens of Miriam" he coughed. "As your new mayor, it gives me great pleasure to recognize the efforts of these children over the years. They have cleaned up this neighborhood and attracted new business, petitioned for a bookmobile so that the library could reach even more patrons, and fought for multiracial hiring practices at Sunrise, which held to the hire of Maya Bennett, the school's first black teacher."

He grimaced as applause filled the air.

"In recognition of their service to this community, they have been given the Miriam Good Citizenship Award. So please join me in a round of applause for the Starlight League!"

Midway through the audience, a tall, black man in faded blue jeans frowned deeply. He sported a well kept Afro and a stern, shaven face. He was exceedingly strong but his eyes routinely frightened people more than anything else. They were coldly logical. Unlike most, he never bothered to temper justice with mercy, which is why many called him Thanatos, the name borne by Death in mythology.

"He opposed the hire, the bookmobile, and aid to Weeping Willow, but shamelessly used those policies to get elected as mayor. Now he'll attempt to reverse the progress many of us are fighting for. Well, justice is colorblind" he mumbled darkly, and he walked through the crowds, and out of sight.

December 13, 1960 was a grim evening. At 8:30, plumes of ash and smoke tore through a medium-sized white house on Greenwood Avenue, where Daniel lived. A moment later, Aries burst through the front door, half coughing, and half screaming. Twenty minutes later, Greenwood's residents stood on the threshold of the Miriam police department demanding justice.

Several neighbors had seen a police car in the vicinity before hearing the explosion. and Aries claimed she saw and officer fleeing from the scene. They were rebuffed, and their claims were dismissed as ridiculous, but a small investigation began the following week. When it was completed, Harper was quoted in the Miriam Daily Voice as saying, "Let these baseless charges against our fine police department be laid to rest. No evidence has been found to tie any of our brave officers to the crime."

"That's because cops don't rat each other out!" Thanatos growled, hurling the pages to the ground. "No outside investigators, no consideration of eyewitness testimony, no consideration of the racist beliefs of many of the officers, no consideration of anything. Everyone knows it was the Fieldswallow boys. But they're officers so they're Scott free. The fireworks store said they knew what those explosives were being bought for. What no one knows yet, is justice will be done."

As darkness set over the Jennings Apartments, none could have guessed that Miriam's destiny had been forever altered. Thanatos crept into the shadows of a bedroom to await the morning.

Weeks later, Crystal was still consoling Aries. The two had become inseparable, like sisters. They were often held up as examples of the coming racial harmony, but Aries cared little about that anymore. Whenever she allowed her mind to stray, it turned to her mother, and the hateful people that had killed her. So she dove headfirst into her Starlight League work, and it soon reached the level of obsession.

The death affected Daniel in another way. He had considered his system perfect. He had dared to imagine that a good enough plan could supersede hatred and bring peace and order. The murder of Aries' mother proved him wrong, and he began to reconsider his tactics. Suddenly, instead of just focusing on community service, he began to advocate hate crime awareness. At first, this seemed innocuous to everyone, but when the rhetoric turned against the mayor, whose administration had become known among people of color for publicly supporting civil rights but privately weakening their effect, Harper fought back in ads and at speeches, saying that Daniel and his friends were hypocrites.

"When I began the Starlight League some time ago" Harper opined gravely, "I hoped to give the Negroes some chance of improving themselves. Yet, after all that has been achieved, they accuse my fellows and I of deception, conspiracy, and worse. And these noble gentlemen have said to me, "Leeland, why continue in such futile pursuits. Consider the treatment you have borne, and be quit of this silliness." But I have continued because a father must continue, no matter how unruly the child becomes."

Statements like these soon divided the League from many of its white members, and the support of most of that sector of Miriam. The triumphs of the past, as they often are, had been swept up in the winds of an old man's lies. Though diminished, the group refused to die, and they continued bringing food, books and joy to the homes on and around Weeping Willow Lane.

The seventh anniversary of Maryland's first day of integration was not a celebrated event. This was due mainly to the tragedy that befell Miriam that day. Dissatisfied with the police investigation, Thanatos had decided drastic action was needed to awaken the city. He had planned his "justice" for some time, and on that grim afternoon, the city lost someone who could not be forgotten or swept away.

At 2:33 that day, Aries screamed louder than she ever would again as bullets tore through Crystal's body. They had stood on the library's threshold, taking turns reading aloud to a small group of children. Tears ran down her cheeks as screaming children scattered in all directions. Aries knelt, clutching the body of the girl who had become her closest friend.

Her mother's death rang fresh in her mind, and she wept bitterly as tears mixed with blood.

"You cannot continue this!" Patricia insisted when she heard the news. "Courage is one thing but I will not let you die!" But Daniel was incorrigible. Whenever he could escape his mother's eye he and the League paraded through the city, calling the mayor a disgrace and petitioning for his dismissal. The death, as planned had greatly shocked Miriam's white citizens, and they were lending support to the measure.

"I cannot allow this to continue!" Harper barked as he paced through his office a week after the funeral. The following day, the Voice carried this proclamation:

Resolved: That the organization known as the Starlight League has strayed
from its mission of service and aid to embrace practices which imperil its
membership, mislead the citizenry and hamper the effectiveness of law
enforcement. Now, therefore I, Dr. Leeland Aaron Harper III, Mayor
of the State of Maryland, with the advice and consent of all relevant
authority, do cause all activities of the said organization to cease, and
declare it illegal within the jurisdiction of this state.

The people stopped fighting then, except for Aries who several times tried to illegally revive the Starlight League, and Daniel, who spent most of his days in bitter seclusion. Thanatos was found, identified as John Turner, and sentenced to death. Time passed and the loss was forgotten. The city blossomed in the coming years. But Aries would never be the same. She swore she would be like Crystal. She would comfort the lonely and drive them toward perfection.

On the day Daniel turned eighteen, Virgil and Patricia drew him from his exile. Now was the time for him to begin his formal training so he might one day run the bank. Daniel wanted none of it, and within an hour's space, he vanished from sight, and to the horror of the Rivulets, never returned. He had twice failed his friends, his organization and his city, and repairing that fault consumed his mind. He would think of nothing else in the time that was to follow, but he knew someday he would lift the stain.

Extra Chronicle Two

Amanda

"State your name!" a clear, stern female voice ordered. Across from her, wispy and unsure, the answer came:

"Judith Noelle Miller."

The woman smiled smugly but kept her voice firm.

"You are not Judith Miller. You are Amanda Millicent Woods. If you lie to me again, you will be punished. Do you understand?" Very slowly, the little girl nodded as tears began to form in her radiant green eyes.

"Very well then" the woman replied, "who are you? What is your name?" The girl looked distressingly at the small, black loafers her inquisitor wore beneath a sensible pair of slacks and a long, white lab coat. Three tears splashed on the shoes as, quaking fearfully, she replied.

"I'm...I'm Judith" she breathed pleadingly, beginning to cry, "Judith Miller. I live in Washington DC. My address is..." But she never got to finish because the woman encircled her waist and lifted the girl to her eye-level.

"Now you listen to me, you little pain in the neck" she yelled fiercely. "Your name is Amanda. Not Judith. Amanda. This little fantasy of yours ends right now, or else I'll..."

But at that moment, the door opened, and the raven-haired nurse turned in time to see a clear-eyed, square faced young doctor sporting neatly cropped brown hair. Yawning lazily, as if he was bored by the effort of moving, the intruder raised his hand regally and, looking at the woman, spoke in slow, idle tones.

"That will do, Willamina. Please deposit one little girl on the nearest patch of floor." Willamina released the girl, who landed on her feet with a soft thud.

"We seemed to have achieved the desired result" she remarked, and promptly left the room. The doctor and the little girl were left alone in a small, windowless room containing only a functional sofa and a small coffee table. They sat together, and he began to ask her a series of questions.

Two weeks ago the weepy little girl, who was indeed named Amanda Woods, lay in an off-white machine that seemed to combine an MRI scanner and Snow White's glass coffin. Her robin egg blue hospital gown had wrinkled in several places but the little girl was so tightly encased that adjustments were rendered impossible. She shivered badly, feeling entombed, and unable to hear or see the doctor that stood at the control panel. Carefully examining the controls, the square faced man, Dr. Aaron Lorr, pushed three buttons in rapid succession.

Instantly, Amanda's faced pinched into an unholy agony, and her fists collided with the glass. Her eyes rolled violently in her head as silent screams escaped her lips. Just as she thought the terrible pain would kill her, it was gone. She suddenly felt pleasantly warm and surprisingly cheerful. Dr. Lorr released the glass lid of the machine and it slid away, allowing Amanda to sit up. She did so, smiling brightly, and asked for her mother. Amanda was an orphan. That had been the first evidence that their efforts to create a specific alternate personality in their test subject were bearing fruit.

Amanda Millicent Woods was born in one of Miriam's busier correctional facilities early in 1990. She never knew her mother, who died in the process of giving birth, or her father, who had long ago vanished. The city placed her in the care of Morgan Woods, a bitter old woman, who gave the child her name, and little else. The very instant Amanda turned one, Morgan hauled her into a standing position.

"Quit crawling and walk like you're supposed to!" she cried, releasing the child carelessly. Amanda fell dozens of times and cried incessantly before finally learning to walk a week later.

If she cried for too long, she was spanked. By her second birthday, Amanda was quiet as a mouse no matter what happened.

At five, when she began to show signs of multiple personalities, Morgan cast Amanda from her house, offering the explanation that "it's cheaper this way." A month later, emaciated, plastered with rags and chattering nosily, Amanda did not think twice about entering an unmarked van whose occupants offered her food and shelter. The moment she did, however, the world went black.

Dr. Lorr carefully inserted a hypodermic needle into a guiding sleeve he had earlier driven into Amanda's skull. She had felt very little pain so far, but that was about to change. When the needle had cleared a path, the doctor inserted an electrode to a certain depth in the brain.

"It begins" he murmured seriously, and activated the device. Violent convulsions seized the five year old's frail body. Lorr watched stoically as her head whipped about and her teeth rattled. When Amanda resembled nothing more than a fish out of water, violently flopping and struggling for air, Dr. Lorr silenced the machine and, injecting the child with a sleep inducing chemical, left her to a looped recording of a happy little girl named Judith.

Judith Miller, aged five, was happy indeed. She wasn't hungry, unloved or in dire pain. Instead she giggled happily in the arms of her mother as her father told the story of Jack and the Beanstalk, complete with a deep voice for the giant. Weakened by sleep, and traumatized by the shocks, Amanda's brain began to sop up the tape loops and soon, every time she was exposed to pain, it was blocked from her memory as the alternate personality of Judith rose to control.

Amanda was seven now, and had as many personalities. One reverted her to mental infancy and caused her to place all her hopes in the hands of her doctors. Another brought her great terror and could be used to elicit obedience. A third caused her to do great harm to herself and could be used to keep her from revealing the work Dr. Lorr had done. Still another made her love the doctor unconditionally, despite the tortures he put her through. Amanda was no longer a little girl. Now she was a collection of people that comprised a precisely made weapon.

But that weapon needed testing. Especially the Judith alter. Doctors Willamina Bride and Aaron Lorr worked out of Salvere Hospital for the Mental Energy Research Institute. The Institute had a great interest in Judith and another child that had not been explained to them. It was, however, made perfectly clear that only a perfect copy of Judith would do. So each day, Dr. Bride drew out the alter and tried her best to convince the girl she was Amanda. But every time, her memory of the previous inquisition blocked, she faithfully insisted she was Judith Noelle Miller. One night, late in her eighth year, that assertion would be tested.

As the real Judith Miller was captured by MERI operatives, a single scream escaped her lips. By the time Aries arrived, however, a new child occupied Judith's bed. She had been subjected to cosmetic surgery to look like Judith, tape loops and reprogramming to sound and act like Judith, and as her aunt questioned her, she noted all Judith's injuries, though most seemed to be healing. And Ms. Washington unknowingly accepted her new niece, as did all of Miriam. And Amanda's new personality soon became the only one allowed to shine.

The Story Continues…

Three years have passed and Miriam is in chaos. Suspicion is the order of the day and no one feels safe, leas of all our heroes. They have abandoned their cave for a more hospitable hiding place but new challenges wait in the wings. Can the children survive the wrath of MERI, resolve their differences and find their friends? Find out in the next Chronicle of the Sacred Rulix Crystal:

Tabithia

Coming Soon

Also coming to

The Pocket Revolution:

Extra Chronicle Three

The Black Garden

Forced into the shadows of a hidden cave, an unlikely handful of survivors must eke out an existence, remain alive, and, above all, refrain from killing each other. This is the harrowing story of the bitter aftermath of MERI's first purge. As a fear-stricken city is rocked by violence, it is up to three little girls to set things right. But the Shades are still out there, savagely hunting every Element they can find. And what about Alexander? Can he be saved? Find out in The Black Garden.

Coming Soon

to

stores.lulu.com/thepocketrevolution